PRAISE DANCER'S STORY

Their Life Becomes Their Dance

TERRENCE G. CLARK

THE GLORY CLOUD PUBLICATIONS

Copyright © 2017 by Terrence G. Clark
Published by: The Glory Cloud publications LLC
PO Box 193, Sicklerville NJ 08081
Theglorycloudpublications.com
Cover Design & Typesetting—Stacey Holloway / Terrence G. Clark
Cover Photography—Stacey Holloway / Dreamstime
Printed by Ingram Sparks
Book Layout—TGC publications

Ordering Information: Contact Terrence G. Clark —- or
The Glory Cloud publications LLC — PO Box 193 Sicklerville NJ 08081

Praise Dancer's Story / Terrence G. Clark —1st ed.
ISBN 978-0-9889866-8-8

Dedication

This book is dedicated to all the godly ladies in my life—firstly, my beautiful wife, Linda (which her name translates) followed by my three lovely daughters—Shadee, Decea, Terae (herself a liturgical dancer), my daughter-in-law—Ayra, three granddaughters—Zekia, My-My (in heaven), Mykala, Zariah Lyn, my precious mother—Phyllis (home in glory) and my dear mother-in-law—Mary, who demands of me like the Madonna of scripture did of her transplanted son.

I would remiss to leave out my godly sister sibs (and sib-in-law) women of faith. A special mention to my sister Lynny, who has committed herself to intercede for me.

Furthermore, grace to all the mighty woman of God (pastors, teachers, ministers, coaches, aunts, cousins, friends) who have impacted my life over the years from Sunday school on up.

And all those women, whom some have gone on (from this life) that which by no chance encounter the Lord allowed me—my life to sow. Some today, to me, are still as daughters, sisters, and mothers. To them, from me, Christ virtue did flow. Unawares at times, and to others purposely to stop the rocks that would be thrown.

Even as the Lord in his earthly ministry was supported by the like. The Lord keep them all through His grace.

—Terrence G. Clark

And David danced before the Lord with all his might and was wearing priests' clothing...Yes, and I am willing to look even more foolish than this, but I will be respected by the girls of whom you spoke!"

—King David (2 Samuel 6:14,22 The Living Bible)

Although some of the portrayals in this story are influenced by real people, all of the non-biblical characters are fictitious.

—Terrence G. Clark

In remembrance of—
"My–My"
Alexis Myra Clark
9.18.2007—6.2.2008

Contents

PRAISE DANCER'S STORY

Their Life Becomes Their Dance

TERRENCE G. CLARK

Helping People To Tell Their Story

Helping Others To Know His

1

The Recital

Thinking About It

"Really, she can't dance a little bit. Miss Corinda knows that, but she's always trying to help somebody."

Tiara stepped back from the mirror in the women's room in Mt Bethel's AME Church. She pulled a loose hair from her eye lids with her left hand, and brushed the remaining attached ones into curl with her right.

"I mean, I'm all for everyone being able to express themselves for the Lord, but if we're a team, and the team is the one being viewed, then you can't use everybody."

Ravene was still primping in the mirror. She heard her best friend fussing, but at the moment she was more concerned how she was going to look after rehearsal. Finally, she answered.

"Tiara, I here you, but we're supposed to be more willing to look past that kind of thing in a church group."

"No," Tiara flapped back, looking at Ravene from both the mirror's reflection and her peripheral. "That's what wrong with church groups. I believe we are supposed to give God our best. Excellence that is. We can't always lump everybody in that same category. Some people need to work out their salvation...in their own house."

"Girl you crazy."

"I'm just saying."

"Why you all primp up anyway? We just going bowling after rehearsal," probed Ravine, checking her cell phone again for the time and any missed texts.

"You never know, smiled Tiara"

"Look at you."

"Excellence girl."

"So, what you doing later anyway?" asked Ravene, probing again.

"I'm thinking about going out to Preefies."

"You still thinking about that? That's a...club."

"Shhhh don't say that in here," interrupted Tiara, erasing part of Ravene's description. "You don't have to be into that...it's just that it's jumping... and something to do."

"Nope... I ain't going. And If I ain't going, you know I'm not letting you go by yourself."

"Tsk... Okay mommy, "responded Tiarra, blowing through her curled bottom lip, fluttering her brushed eyelashes.

"I'll go." From behind the brown door, of the third stall, spoke a low, but quiet voice.

Who's that? Demanded Ravene, softly, but still demanding.

TaWush....Thwirl...shhhhh. The door, on third toilet stall, nearest the wall, opened. Shoulder length, brown auburn, hair draped over a hidden face pushed out, before turning and checking the stall to see if she left anything behind.

"It's just me," said Donjae.

Tiara's face dropped. She turned and looked at Ravene and back at Donjae. The smell of toilet bowl freshener mixed with three other fragrances suddenly became apparent. The medium built girl was wearing Beyoncé's latest scent.

Ravene pulled her bottom lip in under her top teeth.

"I'll go with you," said Donjae again, sheepishly looking at Tiara

Swallowing saliva to wet her throat, Tiara probed back. "Uh Uh, you mean go to Preefies."

"Yeah, I'll go," responded the younger girl for the third time.

"Do you even know what that is?"

"Yeah I do..."

"And I mean your parents... wait how old are you any way."

"I'm twenty-one... Look, I just want to be friends." responded Donjae.

"Hey look I'm sorry... I didn't know you were in here... replied Tiara. I guess I was just a little frustrated with practice."

"Well I thought I was doing better, but your right I could, or as you said I can't dance. Well, at least not as good everybody else on the team. But Pastor Deena suggested I join the dance ministry. She said it would help my praise."

3

All three girl became momentarily silent, internalizing the conversations of the last few minutes. Tiara brushed through the back of her long hair once again. She gritted her teeth and swashed her tongue over her top whites, raised her eyebrows and corners of her mouth at the same time. "Well it looks like we're going to Preefies. Right Ravene, you in."

"Okay. Tiarra... Just an hour... just an hour," responded Ravene, as if Donjae's induction into their circle had changed her point of view.

"Don't we all have to finish the last part of rehearsal?" reminded the new girl.

"And Donjae," consoled Tiarra, "you'll be alright just keep the beat. It's a four count with the last song."

I was the first one there. This was usually the case. I never enjoyed being late and avoided it at all times. I sat, in my seat, outside the auditorium. I could have gone in. I had the key. But there I was, outdoors, enjoying the view.

"Beautiful little shrub garden," I thought. It arced around the stone monument, with the engraved marker and the bench. You could see the design on either side. "So nice of the architect to put it there", I thought. As if it was for me. But it was Janice, in housekeeping, who later added the flowers. Golden hibiscus and blue morning glory were part of her theme, backed by a stage of green clover with little daisies dancing amongst them. And, I could smell honeysuckle ever so faint, but still there. I always had a sensitive nose.

It was the early morning hours of an early summer day. Puffy white clouds filled the sky. The rain had stopped earlier in the morning. Pimples of dews remained on some blades of grass, the flowers in the garden, and on the bench where I sat.

A damp breeze blew past my face. "Ahhhh"....It would be nice if everyone enjoyed simple pleasures like that, I mused. I did and I was enjoying my moment waiting for this day's events to begin. This wasn't a day off. Things were quite busy. I was about to make some changes in the ministry. It was events like this that compelled me to hold back just a little longer.

Tanisha Green was the first of the dancers to arrive. Her mom drove up to the door, under the port, stopped, put the car in park, and looked back at her daughter. She watched her teenager gather and pull to her what she could cradle up into her arms. "Mom." Tanisha looked at her mother believing she knew what she needed without saying it.

"I'll bring the flags in after I park. You got time." her mom responded understandably and assuredly.

The 10th East Coast Liturgical Dance Recital was scheduled for the first Saturday in June. The event had quickly become so popular that the dates and venues were set two years in advance, this one almost before the end of the eighth.

Although, as in its title the event highlighted dance troupes from the eastern part of the US, participants from other parts of the nation, as well as several overseas organizations, still were allowed. The winners from the regionals—east and west, participated in the national event that took place every other year. There were other recitals held all over the States as well as the world. The East Coast was largest whereas recognition was concerned.

There were many in the circle who believed the resurrected dance ministry had started on the east coast. A pioneer drama production team in Glassboro New Jersey was accredited for the spiritual launch. There were others. I knew. I kept up with this kind of thing. Like fire, it's not always where a flame is sparked that started a blaze but where it is fanned.

This was the first year for many of the troupes from the Mideast states, as it was being held this year in South Jersey. Mt. Laurel was the highest point geographically in South Jersey so it made it a fitting place for a summit of any kind.

Over sixty troupes would be here. Participants were selected from applications and from pastoral recommendation. Each group had to represent a church, Christian dance school, or a dance school that had a Christian program. There would have been a whole lot more but not every dance troupe had the money or time to attend. I didn't like it, but registration was a hundred dollars. And, it was of course first come, first served, plus a list of other qualifiers—team performance, as well as individuals. The day started at eight. The first dance was at nine, following the worship, prayer, opening dedication, and reading of rules. Each team or individual got five minutes or less. Although, depending on the song, allowance might be made. Friday evening was the early bird, so a few ministries were allowed to go forth then.

This wasn't supposed to be a dance competition. It was birthed to be a display of ministry and worship to God. This was always stressed in the opening ceremony and clearly highlighted in the brochures and registration material sent out to over two-hundred potential teams. Most of the dancers knew it. "We come to worship God" was the motto, mission and mantra. But the chance to show off some talents and skill hard to silence.

Tanisha read the pamphlet over and over again. She swallowed hard when the head of the dance ministry handed out the information and talked about the possibility of *Fellowship Worship Center* going this year. She loved to dance. She remembered, as early as three-years-old, standing in front of the hallway mirror twirling and sashaying. When Pastor Steve finally gave the okay to allow dance ministry in their church, it was the first time she saw people dance for the Lord.

The songs came alive she thought. And she could see herself swirling and twirling upfront and on stage. She threw her arms back in a high praise and turned around three times just as her mother came in.

"Ah...I see the praise dance has got your attention," commented her mother Karen while stretching, squinting her eyebrows, and smiling slightly.

"Do you think they'll let me join at nine? Is there and age limit?"

"I'm not sure. But let's find out. As much as you love to dance, I am sure they'll make a way."

There wasn't an age limit. But they did want commitment.

"It's not just dancing. It's ministry," shared Sister Henrietta at the introductory meeting. Pastor Steve wanted that to be emphasized first and often.

Tanisha knew about the Word and church, but she really didn't know what ministry meant. Pastor Steve was a minister. Would she have to dress like Pastor Marcie—Pastor's Steve wife? Would she have to talk proper all the time? She loved her church's pastor but thought sometimes the way he talked sounded funny. He would draw out his words.

"Weeee are here today...too magnify the Lord," was how Sunday morning sermons usually started. It was as if his brain was getting warmed up. It was strange talking, but it was still kind of interesting. It made folks to expect what he was going to say next, even though his opening was usually one of several usual phrases.

The sermons were one thing, Tanisha thought, but when he talked to people directly, sometimes he still spoke differently. Not so much a drawl, but more so trying to talk cool to the kids. "Hiiiii my young sista. You been praising the Lord?"

And although the mid-aged pastor laughed a lot. It still seemed like he was such a serious man.

"Perhaps it's too much to compare myself to Pastor Steve," thought Tanisha, "but does serving God mean I can't play at the park or watch TV. Do I have to read my bible all the time?"

Tanisha wasn't sure. But, she was sure, she wanted to dance. And dancing for the Lord seemed good, and the opportunity was there in front of her.

She was fifteen now. The church danced team had grown too. Some people had come and some people had left. Being there since the beginning, her talent was honed tight. To hit that artistic level, she had added ballet, jazz, and some tap dance steps to some of her routines.

"That girl dances like an angel," her church members would say. Like an angel was not what she really wanted to hear. That was nice, but she thought that limited her. She wanted her dances to express things that were in her. Things she felt as a young girl—hurts, disap-pointments, hopes, fears and relationships. Dancing was her place of expression. She could talk there and explain things. She could hear, see, and imagine things. Some things she had never seen or done before.

The last notes of Tamela Mann's *Take Me To The King* were gloriously resounding. Tamika Whitsetter imagined angels dancing before God and in the Garden of Eden. She loved it when Tanisha danced imagining that she learned her technique from Belinda—the imagined name of the one assigned to her. Her mother agreed often calling Tanisha—Miss Angel.

Fellowship Worship Center's dance program was like many other churches. Mostly young girls joined—early teens through mid-teens, thirteen to seventeen. The ages skipped and went to thirty to forty-five after that. The thought, the young adults were now either finding their way through school, college, finding a job, or marriage and starting new family.

The twenty-year-olds were passing the stage where they needed to show themselves. The need for approval gained from other people, sometimes sensed after an audience applauded their performance, waned to self-discovery. The idea of being God's little flower or angel was challenged. Womanhood called. Later the still quiet voice of the Heavenly Father would once again be heard when they realized that life apart from Him was rather empty. Husband or boyfriend could not alone satisfy, and the longing to dance for Him returned. Dancing was always to tell the story, but by mid-thirty, some disappointments and triumphs experienced in life, then made it easier to tell. The younger sisters, with an exception of those like Tanisha, treated dance as cheer club, and were able to release their youthful energy. For many churches dance was a great way to give the kids something to do. So, the concept of a church dance and cheer squad, apart from the liturgy, was still an okay idea.

Ms. Connelly was at the registration table, in the foyer, meeting the girls as soon as they walked in. She folded a piece of paper and put it to the side for later. She knew someone was coming in the door following the slight chill.

Her eyes rescanned the table assuring the registration tags in front of her, were still there. Looking up she smiled real big at Tanisha who was coming in, bumping her stuff against the door as she entered. It was evident, this first arrival was somewhere between enjoying being there and nervous at the same time.

"Welcome young woman of God to *The Tenth East Coast Liturgical Dance Recital.*"

Tanisha smiled back, recognizing Ms. Connelly from last year, but not remembering her name.

"Good Morning, am I the first one here?"

"Yes," the middle-aged, dark brown skinned, woman smiled back. "And that says a lot for you. Being early, you must be ready to give your best to God."

Tanisha didn't respond. Although she was touting confidence. A sense of competitive dominance surfaced in her. She thought, "If what Ms. Connelly said is true, being early could only serve competitively and give me an edge."

Another chill entered the foyer. Two younger girls entered, pushing the thick glass door with them, followed by their mother who looked more like their sister. Janivera and Jantasha were twins. Nine years old. Their first year at the recital. They weren't nervous. In fact, they were rather confident. All they knew was practice, know your steps, have fun, praise God, and act professional—like Gabby (Douglas). That's what their mother Justine Janiver taught them. Tanishsa picked up her registration. Out of the corner of her eye she spied the two sisters. She thought, "So this is the competition." Later she would feel like a big sister to them.

2

Corinda's Story

Getting Free

Corinda stretched out face down across her bed, folded her arms out in front of her, and cradled her forehead in them. It had been a long day. She ran down through the activities of the day starting with the morning.

"Three fights today that's unusual, I know it's a secular school, but the kids..."

She heard the crunch of springs and mattress at the same time she felt the weight of her husband quickly, but gently, come down upon her, until his head, face and cheek nestle against hers. The smell of the cologne he wore during the week, and the warmth of his body soothed her like an aromatic candle, filling her nostrils all at once. She smiled and paused her thoughts, letting the days stress escape like the air from the mattress.

"Hey babe, how you doing?"

Barry spoke first, and then he paused, lifted and turned his head, kissed her cheek and then her head. He started to get up as if he had something else to do. Corinda reached her hand back, grabbed his belt from the side, and gently but firmly pulled him back down onto her body.

"No don't get up. I need you as a comforter about right now."

Barry settled back down on his wife, kissing her head again and then her cheek this time, before repositioning the side of his face next to hers.

"So how are you doing?" Emphasizing the words individually this time and dragging out the word—so."

"I'm good, just a long day. The kids were a little antsy today."

"I know you'll be glad when retirement comes."

"I don't know. I like what I do. You know that. I like being able to impute into the kids. It's just the other stuff. Sometimes I think it's the parents more than anything. You know a lot of these kids are dealing with issues from home. They're acting out."

"Yeah, but baby, thirty years of that would drive me crazy."

"But it hasn't always been this way," sighed Corinda. "It used to be the racial things, getting the black kids to feel they fit in and they could learn just as well as the white counterparts. And then, it was dealing with poverty issues. Kids fighting hunger pangs trying to focus on school work. The free lunches and meal allowance seemed to have dealt with half that. Now it's the sexual issues and video game violence. You can't tell me these kids aren't getting some of their promiscuous and violent behaviors form video games."

"I hear you babe. So why don't we do something tonight?" Barry proposed, subtlety changing the subject. "Dinner... a movie? We can take a ride to AC and walk the boardwalk."

"You forgot. It's dance ministry tonight... We're getting ready for the big recital in June."

"That's tonight?" surprisingly responded Barry.

"Tuesdays and Fridays until after the Recital then back to every other Friday."

"Now that's a class I know you don't have any problem with." Barry bantered, hoping his wife didn't catch his sarcasm.

"Baby you know that's what I'm called to do. And the kids, as well as the adults, are there because they want to. Everyone is on one accord."

"Everyone?" Pushed back Barry.

"Well you know. But at least everyone's focused for the event. I am really blessed to see how they have progressed especially Donjae Brown and Patty Rodriguez, who would have ever thought. Anyway, I can lay here another five minutes and then..."

"Nope," interrupted Barry as he lifted his head and pushed his body up with one hand. Throwing his left leg off the side of the bed and purposely pushing the rest of the way up by using his wife's behind as a stabilizer. "You missed that one. Let me let you get yourself together so you can get ready for this evening."

Emphatically, Corinda's husband smiled but at same time he felt a little left out. He totally supported his wife's ministry but sometimes he hoped she would just spend time with him. He would never tell her that. More so, he would never let on that he sometimes thought God was his competition.

Corinda sunk back in the bed and looked for where she left off in her review of the day. Her eyes lifted and caught the sight of the black screen of the television across the room.

"You had enough. How much of this are you going to smoke girl?" She pushed back into David's arms as they sat in the car. Smoke filled the inside—a mixture of marihuana and incense. They had smoked two joints and drank several beers. David's car was parked in back of Eckerd's Park hidden in the trees pass the picnic tables.

Corinda laughed and turned her face toward David's blowing smoke into his face. She turned to him, pulled her body up on his, until her lips were close to his, and kissed him. Her face changed. Her rose blushed cheeks and peachy skin turned a shade of green. She was sick—throwing up on him.

"Ahhhh Crap," David hollered pushing her off. "Look what you did."

"Easy baby I'm just sick."

By the time David got her home, he had cooled down. With his face turned slightly to the left, towards the open window, the smell of vomit was tolerable. "You alright girl?"

"I don't know. I feel weak. I think I need you to help me to the door."

"To the door, ain't your Dad home?"

"I'm not sure. But it's okay," grunting as she talked."

David was worried more about her Dad than getting her to the house safe. Unknown to him, Mr. Clemons was working late shift that night. He wasn't home.

"Just get me to the door and leave," she whispered.

David helped Corinda to the door. She leaned on him until he transferred her balance to the door arch. Hurried he steadied her and slipped back to his car, still wondering if her father was home. He paused until the front door shut, put the car in gear and left.

Corinda stumbled into the living room and fell on couch. Only to jump up and run to bathroom when her inside seemed to want to come out again. She barely made it to the toilet. Bent over, clutching the seat with her hands, she stared into the bowl, examining her stomach contents for a moment.

"What did I have tonight? Man that stuff tore me up. I can't keep doing this."

The twenty-one year old, sophomore college student had a lot going for her, but she now was about to mess it up. She lifted hers head to the sink, turned the water on, cupped her hands, filling them with water, sucked it into her mouth, and spit it out. She leaned on the counter and stared at herself in the vanity mirror.

"I look really bad." She pulled some missed vomit from her hair. She thought about David. "David's a nice guy, she thought, but I don't know where this is going, or where it should be going."

She met David after dance class. Her major was education, but she minored in dance. It would have been the other way around, but counselors told her it was hard to get into a professional dance career and better to have the teaching to fall back on.

David was in the student lounge after class. Their eyes met and they introduced themselves. One thing led to another and it wasn't long before she was his girl. They laughed about it. They were an un-likely couple. He didn't even dance. She loved to dance. What he loved to do was get high. So he turned her on to Marijuana, alcohol and sex.

She should have listened to the warning signs when, at her last competition, she missed step and twisted her ankle. She never told anybody she missed the step because she felt dizzy. Corinda's thoughts were interrupted by voices coming from the living room. "Daddy's home...Oh No," she thought. Quickly shutting the bathroom door, before cautiously cracking it open, she looked out to see if she could see her father. When she couldn't, she pulled the door further open, and stuck her head out.

It wasn't her father. It was the TV. "I don't remember that being on when I came home. Then again as sick as I was I don't remember."

She looked around again; making sure her father wasn't stand-ing there, waiting for her to come out. She headed back to the couch. A television evangelist was on. "What's this Billy Graham or some-body?"

She was about to turn it off when it happened.

"Are you sick and tired of being sick and tired?"

"Cliché," she thought, "these preachers always speak in clichés."

She reached her hand out to turn it off again.

"God is talking to you right now."

She knew the preacher was being rather general in his state-ment. Anybody could be watching. It was funny thing, though. At that moment, if was as if she could hear God talking to her. Setting down side ways, in the corner of the sofa, leaning on her right arm and hand, with her legs drawn to her, she listened to the preacher's charismatic clichés strung together one after the other.

"Jesus Christ gave his life for you. God so loved the world that he gave His son to you. This is not an accident that you are watching. Give your life to Jesus now."

The preacher then led Corinda Clemons, and whoever else was watching, listening and responding, in the "Sinner's Prayer". That night, Corinda's life was changed.

3
Juanita

The Temple

"Girl let me tell you, if the mayor knew. If those people knew what was about to happen in this city. Please. I mean those other groups have been getting funding for years. We have these girls.

Yes, this is a faith based organization. Okay we know it's Christian based. Okay it's Christ based. But they have to understand that the Christian community is a viable community and just as worthy to receive funding as any other.

More so...who can say we aren't raising up young women, young people, who are going to positively affect the community with solid wholesome values? I am tired of these other groups taking things away in the name of faith based initiative.

I mean look at Candy. God knows that woman is an example of Christian accomplishment. And I don't believe she still fully gets the recognition. The sister should be CEO of a major company not just the COO. And the most of the city of Camden don't even know her accomplishments.

These are the kind of people that need to be out in the forefront. These are the young women and men that should be on the mic, at the podium, at the rallies, guest in the churches speaking to our youth. Well look, I have to go. Somebody's at the door. "

Juanita Simons-Williams had been the principal and superintendent at Campbell's Kings School for Gifted Girls for fifteen years. She had held several positions including tenth grade history teacher, guidance counselor, assistant principal and now the head position. Still, it wasn't just a job to her. She enjoyed what she did. She loved the girls.

The Camden school never seemed to get righteous recognition. The stats were always swallowed up in the negative news about the city. But not just the stats, of the girl that had graduated from the school, eighty-eight percent went on to careers that were making a difference around the globe. One of these hopefuls now stood at her door—Zeesia Lothens an honor student. Nodding her head, with the phone seemingly attached to her ear, she hurried her last thought with her longtime friend Enid Winslow.

"Yeah, you know girl this keeps me fired up. Got to. Somebody's *got to* look after our community and our young people. Alright Miss Enid, I'll talk to you later. Oh, and about what you called about, tell my friend Mr. Randy, it's okay to use the park for his event. He still needs to fill out the paperwork. Alright girl, I will talk to you later."

Miss Juanita had a dark chocolate complexion that seemed to warm up like hot cocoa when she talked to her girls. She was stern, but had a warmth when she communicated with them. Even the girls with the most challenging backgrounds could listen to and receive from her.

"Hi Miss Zee." (Zee is what a lot of people called Zeesia.) Miss Zeesia is what a lot of her teachers called her. But Miss Juanita really smiled and emphasized her name the most.

"Miss Juanita, can I talk to you? You said we could come to you when we had challenges."

"Sure Miss Zee, come on in," said the principle, standing behind her desk while closing folders. "Door open or door shut. By the look on your face, it looks like you want the door shut."

"Do you want to sit down?"

"Yes Ma'am."

The school superintendent, student counselor, and to some—god-mother pointed to the black vinyl, covered, chair in front of her desk. Zeesia moved between the chair and polished wood-grain desk and slowly sat down.

Campbell invited talented and deserving girls from the city and the county. Other girls were sometimes allowed from other counties in the Garden State. Some of the young ladies matriculated from other institutions. Campbell's wasn't registered as a Christian school. It was listed as faith based, meaning it had to raise most of it money via funding and donations from the private sector.

The board kept pushing for the school to seek after government initiatives. Superintendent pushed against the ideas for years. She knew to receive government initiatives the school would have to drop some, if not all, of their Christian based curriculum and atmosphere.

The girls began the day with prayer. There was a morning assembly where they all met in the auditorium and Mrs. Thatch—the school chaplain—led in prayer, gave the scripture for the day, and sometimes a quote from a Christian or some other right-thinking motivational speaker. She was always quoting Martin Luther King Jr., Maya Angelo, Fredrick Douglas, and Ben Cartwright. Sometimes there would be a quote from Pastor Joel Osteen. Ritualistically, they sing a verse of *I Will Sing of The Mercy of the Lord* before The Pledge of Allegiance to the US Flag. All of that would have to stop. Everything but the Pledge of Allegiance.

Miss Juanita direction was to just keep believing God and stay in constant communication with companies and churches. Every little bit helps. There were some allocations from the government—bare minimum, some subsidies, as the school was providing a form of scholastic education. And, the parents contributed also. Girls could win scholarships, but the most of the girls who went to Campbell their families were well to do. At least better than many of their urban counterparts.

Zeesia's father, Melvin Lothens, was a Philly lawyer—a corporate business lawyer. Her mother, Dr. Margi Hodges-Lothens, was a dentist in Mt Holly NJ. Their 17-year-old daughter was extremely gifted. Zeesia showed the propensity for science in preschool. At least that's how her parents interpreted her long staring at objects—mechanical and biological. They proposed that she was trying to figure out how they worked. They must have been right. Her aptitude in math and science soared above her class mates in elementary school. She was reading on a college level in eight grade.

It was Margi who suggested Campbell for her little prodigy. She went there. She knew the curriculum and she knew Juanita Simmons. Surprisingly Melvin Lothen didn't want his daughter to leave public school. He felt she needed the social impact it provided. The truth was he thought the development process of a specialized institution would cause his little girl to grow up to fast. It wasn't that Margi had the last say in the family, but she was the most persuasive, despite the fact of Melvin being an attorney.

"Miss Zee, I know I don't have to pull your files. Academically, I knew you are doing great. I am so glad your mother and father allowed you to attend here three years ago. I love all you girls here. But, don't tell anyone. You know that you are one of my favorites. So, what's going on in that strong, beautiful, young, black temple?"

"I love science as you know and that's my major. I'm going for it."

"First black sister to win a Nobel Peace Prize in a hard science," said the two educated black women together, as if they had rehearsed the line several times.

"But there's more," continued Zeesia. "You, this school, along with my parents, taught us to pray...to always seek God about everything. Lately, I have been waking up around two every morning. I wake up praying. I mean tears are running down my face. I asked the Lord what was going on. I mean, it wasn't scary. In fact, I felt closer to God then I ever did. I could sense his love like he was right there. Right there holding me."

"So what did he say when you talked to him?" queried Miss Juanita.

"He wants me to dance."

"Dance?"

"Yes he wants me to dance—like praise dance—liturgical dance," answered her student.

25

"I can see you doing that girl. You can do that" responded the Principle, adjusting her thoughts, because she didn't here Zeesia say she was dispelling her other pursuits.

"I can see it. You can see it. But you know my mom, she won't see it. If it's not science or math, she doesn't want me involved. You know how she thinks. She'll say, 'Leave that to other girls, that's all they got. God gave you a brain. You don't need to do that.'"

Miss Juanita smiled. Her eyes brows stretched to mid forehead. "I know that Margi. But you can dance anywhere right. Did the Lord mean in a church service?"

"Well," said Zeesia, looking over her nose at Ms. Juanita. "I believe he wants me to minister at the East Coast Dance Recital competition in June."

"Really...Have you danced before?"

"No...I mean messing around or in my private worship. I twirl around. I never really had an inclination to dance publicly before. Definitely not as a ministry."

"Hmmmm...well, one thing I know for sure," smiled Miss Juanita, "if God told you to do it, and you know it's him, you have to do it."

"I know. How do you think I should approach my mother?" asked Zeesia.

"Well straight and direct...with a lot of conviction has always been my Modus Operandi. And, the other wonderful thing we know about doing something for God, if He really told you to do it, then he will provide. And, he will make the way. He convinced Pharaoh. Esther convince King Xerxes, and your mother always convinces your father." Miss Juanita smiled. "I shouldn't say that to you. But you know."

"Yeah I know," smiled Zeesia.

"Margi Lothens may be a master of persuasion when it comes to her family, but she's no match for the Holy Spirit," responded Miss Juanita looking almost crossed-eyed across her desk, focusing her gaze directly at Zeesia, while sucking her left upper lip in. It was an indication that everyone knew that she was driving her point home. It was still funny. It was as if it was the last line of a stage play, before the curtain closed. Miss Juanita knew it too. They both laughed.

The applause waned to several hand claps before the silence. The Emcee called the next name. They would dim the lights as each girl took the stage. Zeesia took her pose, waiting still, and patient, for her music to play, listening for her cue. Her legs were crossed. Right leg out front, toes in point, left arm up high next to her head, bent at the elbow, and resting a half inch over her head.

"You deserve the glory."

The first line following the eighth chord.

"And the Honor"

The song expressing the glory of the most high.

Zeesia danced. Tears flowed. The young scientist to be was dancing a story of the glory of God. It was a story of how great God was. All that she had learned academically was engulfed in the presence of the Almighty.

I was there on the front row. I had seen her dance before. But not liked this. I could feel her presence and hear the song. It was like what I always said, "The dance must tell the story."

Melvin Lothen was sitting to my right. He pulled out his handkerchief secretly wiping his eyes as his daughter ministered. I knew something was breaking inside of him. He hadn't told anybody. He was always fearful that he would be suddenly taken away from his family. The worry of that had begun to pervade in his mind. Before it was just a thought, but lately it had surfaced to a harassment. Today as his little girl danced and ministered to the Lord all the fear and worry of his family lifted. He smiled, dabbed his eye again with his handkerchief, and was free again.

Margi was not there, it wasn't because her daughter was dancing. She was out of town, in Las Vegas, at a dentist convention. She accepted the dancing idea with less resistance than anyone thought. The truce was 'this dancing' as she said could not interfere with Zeesia education. Dancing was still extracurricular to her, although she knew it was for the Lord. Zeesia agreed and now here she was.

4
Dorie

All My Life

Carl loved his little Dorie and that's what everyone knew. They pulled into the church yard every Sunday morning at 9:45 like clockwork. Carl still served on the deacon board. He had been there since anyone could remember, although the books listed him back to 1958.

Dories family lived in Nassawadox, Virginia a small town. People from the north mistakenly would assumed that anybody from states below Delaware were country folk. But they never met Dorie. Dorie was five foot five and thinly built. She hadn't changed much in size and stature since she was a teenager.

When she was a young girl, she wanted to go to charm school. She wanted to be like those girls she saw on the screen. *Katherine Hepburn, Jane Mansfield,* and *Eartha Kitt.*

She dreamed of participating in a beauty pageant. Her family lived financially okay for blacks living in that part of the country, but they weren't rich. Dad worked in the factory, but had a part time business selling a specialty brand of skin ointments and food extract. The white folks loved them. The extra helped put them over. Still, they couldn't afford to send her to charm school.

"That would be 25 cents," said Mr. Palmer. Dorie handed him the quarter, pinching it in her fingers and placing it right in the center of his palm, not sliding it across the counter as the other kids did.

"You going to be one of those girls in those magazines?" asked Mr. Palmer.

Yes one day. Although the women in those fashion magazines were white, rosy skinned, and thin lipped. In the years to come, she was excited when black women such as Dorothy Dandridge, Eartha Kits (Catwoman) and Nichelle Nichols (Lieutenant Uhura) appeared on the TV screen. It gave her hope.

Now looking at herself in the mirror she raised her left hand high and dipped to the left side keeping her long thin body straight. She smiled. Staring at her own eyes, she stretched them, trying to reach her temples and watched them pull back into shape. "One day," she said, now cupping her hands over her breast and pushing them up. Giving them some help to accent her frame.

It was an exciting day at the Chadam County Fair. The whole town had come. Blacks and whites at the same events. Not like Sunday morning, when church goers in the town, who were supposedly celebrating the same faith, went to different churches. The air was filled with music mixed with voices from the crowds, the sounds of vendors, the squeaking of the carnival rides, and other mechanical devices turning. Cotton candy and roasted peanuts scents also filled the air. The smell of wet, washed hog and horse hair also crept through the crowds, but nobody seemed to mind

It was 2 PM and time for the contest. Twelve girls had signed up for the pageant. This was Dorie's first. It was her chance. Grams had helped her with her dress. Grams was great with sewing and design. Momma was alright, but Grams could take your idea without even drawing it out and cause what you saw inside to come out for real.

It was a green, satin, full length, gown-like dress that fit her perfectly. It was sexy even though no one really used that term in those days. Still, it was stately. Her arms were bare. Glamorously, it draped down between her neck and shoulders—V necked, exposing just a little cleavage.

Grams made a hat using cardboard as a base. It was same color as the dress. It was a wide brim that radiated three inches from her head over her face. She wore it tilted up allowing her beige skinned face to be fully seen.

"Dorie Carter," called the announcer. "Why do you want to be Miss Chadam County?"

Carmeletta had already answered. Carmeletta was the Mayor's daughter. "I want to help the horses" She explained, "There are horses that are used for food in some countries and I'm going to help end the hurting of horses"

There was a lot of clapping. Some folks didn't know if they were clapping because of what she had said or because she was the mayor's daughter. Carmeltta did look good. She had on a white ruffled dress that rose to her knees. With clear pantyhose that made her look older, but a kid at the same time. Her blonde hair fell long with curls spiraling down each strand.

Dorie swallowed. "I want to help black, Negro, girls to get better education and start their own businesses. But not just black girls, all women and men to be what God wants them to be in life."

There were a couple of hand claps that were finally joined by the rest. Still not as much as Carmeletta.

"And the winner...Dorie Carter." She won. Carmeletta who had won last year placed the Miss Chadam County crown on her head.

Mercie Brant, a black woman, whispered out loud, in surprised, to Casie Lucus. "She won."

Only a few people knew that it was a combination of the statement, the dress, the talent (in which Dorie danced) and the pie eating contest.

"Who is that?" said Danny Coles, as if he didn't see her on stage, in front everyone.

"That's Dorie Carter," said Bennie Willis

"She's fine. I have to talk to her. I believe I'm going to marry that girl one day"

He found his way to Dorie.

Danny died in 1975. He was in a car accident on the way home one evening. A drunk driver—himself, according to the police report. He ran into a tree at high speeds and was apparently killed instantly.

Carl met Dorie in 1980. She was visiting his church. His first wife Lucinda had went home to heaven ten years earlier.

"He noticed her," as he would say as she came around to the offering. In the small Baptist church he served, the members would walk their offering up to the basket as someone held it. Even at fifty Dorie was still stately, attractive, and carried herself like a model. Her bad years with Danny hadn't changed that.

He didn't say anything, but Carl couldn't keep her off his mind. In fact, he just showed up on her door step holding a bouquet of white daisies and some other stuff.

"There's a man out here with a handful of weeds," hollered Sadie, Dorie sister, glancing back to carry the message, but staring back at Carl. She couldn't believe it. Somebody's come to court Dorie. Wilson, Sadie husband came over from the garage when he heard Carl knock.

"You must have come to see Dorie," said Wilson, when he got fifty feet from Carl and still walking towards him. "Sadie's already married and I don't particularly like flowers."

"Yes," said Carl. Laughing as he spoke. "I'm Deacon Henry from Mt. Hope Baptist Church. I was hoping your sister-in-law would go to the races with me."

"Well you have to ask her. It been a while since her husband died," answered Dorie's brother-in-law. He added his second statement as if he needed to reveal the possibility of baggage before anything got started.

Sadie was still standing at the door and pulled back the curtain again to look at the man her husband was talking too. Dorie looked down from the upstairs window. She didn't really remember Carl. Her mind wasn't on men when she visited her sister's church on Sunday.

She didn't go to the race track with him that Friday. They talked in the living room and then under the tree on the white chairs. She went to the race track the next Friday, and the Friday after that. The courtship lasted a year in a half before they were married.

Dorie enjoyed her life with Carl for the most part. He was ten year older than she was. His maturity comforted her assuring more stability than she hadn't known in her past. Other than going to the track races, her new husband was a homebody. Retired, he spent most of time, in the garage, tinkering on small engines—lawn mowers and motor bikes. Carl had a place in Sharonville in the back of an auction house. She never liked it there. It was old.

From time to time thoughts of her past came up. Her lovers shared a passion for car and engines. For reasons unknown and probably why, she was connected with both. With Danny, it was literally life in the fast lane. Danny got a job working with one of the pit crews at a track in Jersey. He loved it. It made him feel important. He loved his orange jumpsuit with the name Tony Ronsalas and the words Pit Crew on the back. The girls loved it too. The little black girls were always looking and commenting on his chiseled forearms that came from doing mechanic work. The white girls also smiled and looked at him out of the corner of their eyes when they walked by. Nonetheless, Danny was faithful. His only lust was for fast cars, speed, and booze. After that it was his love for God and Dorie and in that order.

For Dorie, before Danny, and before Carl, was her dream to be a fashion model. After sixteen years of marriage Carl went home to be with the Lord. She stayed at the old place as long as she could. She finally got a place at West Garden, an independent living facility in nearby Rowanboro not too far from her church.

She loved the church. And now that she was a widow again, she could really give her life to the Lord. And she did, her testimonies were so rich and full of joy.

"She talked about Carl that way," someone noted

Dorie had turned seventy six when First Baptist Church started their dance ministry. She watched the young girls float and move. Their bodies were one with the worship music. She found herself at home again in front of a full-length mirror, arms lifted high, curved back. Her right leg out, toe touching in point.

"I will sing of the mercies of the Lord forever. I will sing" Humming the tune of the eighty-ninth Psalm, she spun and moved rhythmically across the floor. Soon she was a young girl again. She found herself standing before the Father and the room seemingly filled with light.

Friday nights were the practice for the dance ministry. Dorie was there. Her granddaughter Merame drove her. She joined the ministry. There was an awesome anointing, two Sunday later, as she danced across the floor with the team.

"And next, we have dancing for us today is the most senior of our dancers today. Normally I wouldn't give out the ages of the women dancers. And normally they wouldn't let me. But this young lady insisted that I do. Dancing for the Lord at eighty-one and representing First Baptist Church in Rowanboro NJ, Ms. Dorie Henry. Dancing to *His Eyes Is On the Sparrow*."

Dorie just started dancing at eighty. She was bothered with Arthritis. She's been a widow twice. Helped raise her grandchildren. I've known her for years. She and I go way back. I knew her back when she was with Danny. I was one of of the few who knew the real reason why she won the Miss Chatham County Fair pageant. She had asked me to come to-day. She promised that while she was representing many things, as she moved ever so gracefully across the floor, she had dedicated the dance to me. I couldn't say no. I had to be there.

And, I thoroughly enjoyed Dorie's dance. No one else saw it, but I knew, when she had hit 'the moment' and she was a little girl again. I could also see, when she had gone into heaven, and the room became filled with light."

5
Backstage

There Was An Accident

Tamera Jackson performed to the same song that Nessie Smith Colby from Dallas had submitted. Nessie was angry. She couldn't believe that God would have her spend all that time working on a song that someone else was performing.

She couldn't shake her feelings and she was up next. She didn't want to be angry while performing but that was what was about to happen. Thankfully, the emcee announced a ten minute break so the sound techs could change out a mixer. Carrie Wilson from Michigan's Urban League Squad was standing backstage as Nessie went right to left. She would enter on the audience right as instructed. "I guess at least I'll come in from the other side that will be different. No one will see that," she thought. "I'll be standing there when the curtain opens." She was still angry.

"I'm doing the same song too, voiced Carrie. It must be God's will."

Nessie looked back at Carrie while still walking to her destination, slowing down a little to look, without running into anything in front of her. "Are you talking to me?" looking at Carrie not knowing her name.

"Oh me, no I'm just talking to my mother."

Nessie stopped, her eyes searching her fellow dancer up and down, looking for the Bluetooth or cell phone. There was neither.

"Oh, I'm not crazy. Momma's in heaven. I know she's not here, but sometimes I just talk as if she is. I am imagining that Jesus is letting her hear me... and no, she doesn't talk back. I'm not crazy."

"Oh, I didn't say that," choked Nessie. She was thinking something on those lines. And still the thought hadn't left her completely. "You said you're doing the same song. What were you talking about?"

"The girl that just went on two dances earlier, I'm dancing to that song," answered Carrie.

"You mean *Highest Praise*, by *Yalisa Shaboe*?" offered Nessie.

"Yes, that one."

"Well, you're really going to need to talk to your momma," revealed Nessie, raising her eye brows and being slightly sarcastic at the same time, "because that's what I'm dancing to," breathed Nessie. Just releasing the thought, to someone else helped to dispel more of her anger.

Carrie laughed. "Oh Lord, let Momma hear that."

Saying Lord first sounded a little saner to Nessie.

"Look, like I said, Its probably God's will. I'm not changing my song or routine either," settled Carrie.

"I mean, you can if you want to," responded Nessie. Her vocal slightly raised, as if asking as well as telling.

"No, that's was mother's favorite song."

"Mine two," chimed Nessie.

"So, where's your mother?" Carrie asked.

"She's in the audience. She's sitting out there waiting to see me perform."

"Minister, you mean," corrected Carrie.

"Oh yeah, right, minister. I know, minister." In agreement, but slightly perturb that this new acquaintance had to remind her.

"Hey do you want to pray before you go out," asked Carrie, looking right into Nessie's eyes.

Nessie paused before saying yes. She wasn't sure where the prayer could lead. After all, the girl was talking to her dead mother. But there was a peace, so she said okay. The two girls grabbed hands, pausing for a moment, allowing the other to speak. Carrie spoke first. "Father God, in Jesus Name, I pray for my friend.... She paused. "I don't know your name."

"Nessie."

"Carrie," exchanged Carrie. "I pray for my friend Nessie that she will minister before you on the stage and before this audience. Please get the glory in her, and in me, in Jesus name. Let her Momma be blessed."

Nessie continued. "Yes Father and forgive me for being angry and selfish. Bless my new friend Carrie—." She paused making sure that she said Carrie name right. Carrie shook her head in approval. "Lord, let her dance and bring glory to you and this crowd. Let her mother in heaven be blessed, in Jesus name, Amen. Wow, I never prayed that last part before."

"You're funny," smiled Carrie. "What's your mother's name?"

"Sharen."

My mother had a sister named Sharen. I never met her. She didn't come to Momma's home going service."

"Why?" asked Nessie.

"I think she was angry at my mother. She blamed Momma for stealing her fiancé. Momma said it just happened."

"Wow... so do you know where your aunt lives."

"I think somewhere in Texas. Dallas, maybe?"

Juanita Simons-Williams had a blank look in her eyes when she got off the phone.

"What's the matter with you?" asked, LaTanya Mitchell back-stage volunteer and close colleague of Juanita. "You look like you lost your best friend."

"There's been an accident. They tell me Candace's airplane was involved"

"Jesus!" replied Ms. Connelly, who was helping one of the other volunteers line up trophies on a table. "Are you sure? Who called you?"

"My sister Renee has a friend who works for the airport. The plane just crashed on the run way. She said, only the pilot and a flight attendant survived."

Bonnie Himpley, another volunteer who helped direct the dancers onto stage, shaking her head, declared. "Wait a minute. That can't be true. I don't receive that.... Lord Jesus."

"That's what they said."

"What's going on? What's the matter?" Corinda entered the green room to grab some water. It didn't take any special anointing to know something was wrong.

"Candace plane crashed."

"What are you all talking about Candace is on the way here."

"Yes, on the way from Houston. Didn't you know she was away on a business trip?"

"Yeah but..."

"I just got a call. Her plane crashed on the run way only the pilot survived," restated Juanita. I called her cell phone, but she didn't answer.

"Come on...we should pray," acknowledged LaTanya.

"We got to tell the others," suggested Ms. Connelly

"No... Candace wouldn't have wanted that. Wait until the recital is over," encouraged Corinda.

"I don't know...this is pretty serious," challenged Juanita. The school superintendent was a women of faith, but her professional and social instincts surfaced.

"First of all, I think we need to get more information. I'm just not feeling a witness in my spirit. Besides I believe God would have warned us," comforted Corinda. "And on top of that I am believing until the end."

"And, you're right. There's no need to get the girls upset, especially if it's not true," agreed Juanita, while not dismissing the phone call.

"Let pray right now," invited Corinda.

Juanita stretched her hand out towards LaTanya on her left and Ms. Connelly on her right. The others joined in until a circle was form connecting with Corinda who had paused the prayer until they were all together. "I believe God will bring victory in this," she continued.

"Lord let your truth reign in this. We pray and declare that this situation whatever it is—is not unto death but for your glory. Continue to move upon every dancer here today."

"Continue to move upon the people in the audience. So that people will be ministered to. Thank you for your peace upon every dancer and on every one in Jesus name amen."

It wasn't an accident that Carrie and Nessie were ministering to the same song. If they had of looked closer at each other as they exchange conversation, they would have seen the resemblance. They had the same nose and the same lips. It was from their grandfather. It's funny how those things work out. I noticed right away when I saw them.

Everybody didn't know, they were just hoping I'd be there. Unknowingly, I had more involvement than they thought. I saw every application—the girls from last year and all the new performers. I recognized the girl's address right away. I knew background. I had extensive background and education in human resources. I picked up intuitively on people relationships. And, I guess it helped that I knew their grandfather Harry. He was a good friend of mine.

6

Dancing Was Fun

Everybody Dance

Jason stumbled on his way back to Zacharias. He was preoccupied, thinking as he briskly, but hesitantly, walked back to the governor seat. Mathias, the newlywed's father, was his friend, but for this event—his boss. The details of the wedding were ultimately his responsibility. He was usually very resourcefully in calculating every aspect of gatherings such as this, but now apparently, he had failed.

"We are out of wine"

"What?" Replied the thick bearded man, almost splashing out the little he had left in his cup. His attendant quickly reaching out and steadying his hand before it happened.

"I'm sorry. It seems more people are here than the RSVPs."

That may have been true, several of the guest at the reception had originally annulled their invite. People were busy. Jeremiah had just acquired a new yoke of oxen for his farm and was in process of breaking them in. No one was sure why he needed to be there, when he had field help that actually did the work.

Jotham's real estate investment business was taking off and a new plot of land in Nazareth was of interest. He had to go and see it. There wasn't any plausible explanation why on the day of the wedding supper he had to go.

Jeremy and Rachel had just got married themselves. They were still settling in their new house. Although Jeremy's father, according to custom, had given it to them completed. He never really responded to Matthias' invitation requesting his presence to his son and daughter-in-law's big day. However, they all showed up. They and a few others. It wasn't wedding crashing because the weddings of Cana were joyous occasions and people off the streets were joyously welcomed. Mary responded early to her invitation. The messenger at her door quickly confirmed and wrote her name in the book. She was to be accompanied by her rabbi son. At the time, she did not know where he was.

Jesus returned, dirty, scruffy, and skinny after a little over forty days of fasting in the wilderness. He walked through the door and greeted his mother. Physical tiredness had returned. A smile released. He was glad to be home and glad to see his mom. Instinctively, Mary had prepared a waiting meal of veggies, herbs, and yeast bread. Jesus swallowed it down with a cup of goat's milk. He sat down just a moment on the side of the bed, before passing into a much needed deep sleep.

The day of the wedding came several days later. Refreshed, Jesus journeyed with his mother to Cana. With them, desiring to follow him, tagged two of his new acquaintances.

Mary and Mathias were cousins. She hadn't been out to much since her husband Joseph died. This was an opportunity to get back into the community. She had dedicated her widowhood to watching her son. Now he was grown and the head of the house taking care of her. She was still his mother and still anticipating the prophecy. The angel had appeared to her before her and Joseph consummated their marriage. She was pregnant and couldn't explain how, other than what the angel of the Lord had said.

"He shall be called Emanuel—God is with us. He shall save his people. You shall call his name Yeshua—which means Yahweh delivers. He shall bear the government on his shoulders."

Matthias Ben Jesse was the father of the groom. As the custom, the father paid for the great day and feast. This was no cheap event, no expense forfeited. But now, there's no more wine and the party was far from over. So, when Zacharias told him what Jason had discovered, his countenance dropped. Mary was in hearing distance from her cousin. She heard too.

The music was festive, filling the air as if was a natural part of the environment. The band was on key playing continuously. There was dancing everywhere. Mary was looking for Jesus. She found him in one of the circles skipping right to left. The dancers clapping and spinning in unison, laughing and calling out to each other. There was no sensuality in the Jewish circle dances. The flow was praising and thanking Yahweh for all the glorious things he had done and for the blessing of marriage.

"Jesus"

Coming up from behind him and putting her hand gingerly on his shoulder. Mary spoke in that motherly tone that always seemed to be identifiable to their children, despite conflicting sound and whether the kids would admit it. Jesus heard her.

"Yes mother," smiled Jesus, over his shoulder, looking into her eyes.

"They are out of wine"

Jesus kept dancing, but his voice stiffened. He still had a smile, but the look in his eyes changed. "Woman."

He wasn't being disrespectful by calling her that. At once, they both knew what it meant. "What does that have to do with me? My time is not now."

John, one of Jesus disciples, standing by was listening. Mary quickly found Jason. She pointed him to where Jesus was standing. "Whatever he says to do...do."

Jesus was still dancing when Jason approached. He knew about the six clay vessels used for water purification over against one of the walls. "Fill them up with water," said Jesus "and then draw out. Give a cup of it to the governor of the feast."

Jason obeyed. The request was odd. But Jesus spoke with authority. It did help, as Zacharias approached with the cup of what was water, the smell of grapes began to tingle his nose.

"My friend would you please try this and give your blessing."

The bearded man passed the cup under his nose. He didn't know where it came from at first. Jason didn't tell him. He smelled wine. He filled his mouth and swashed it around and swallowed. Mathias wasn't sure where his friend found new wine. He waited for the governor's response.

"This is good. Mathias, I don't know what you did, but you have saved the best wine until last."

It was then Jason told his friend what Jesus had did. The word spread throughout the feast and from there throughout the city. A party had begun.

"Dancing is fun. It was more than the culture. I believe Jesus danced," said the pastor of *Family Life Church* in Collegetown, although in the New Testament, there was no definitive passage that said he did. Pastor Clarence drew his conclusion based on what the Psalms said and how David responded in the presence of God.

"If God said, through David, to dance before the Lord than he sure had to when he was on earth." The senior pastor also taught that some of the Hebrew words for praise in the bible actually meant to dance and to leap. One word—*halel*, means to act clamorously foolish. "And, Jesus went to weddings. I'm sure they danced at the weddings."

Pastor Clarence Claver picked up a broom and made believe it was a guitar. He was gliding on his toes reminisce of a seventy's band from his teenage days. Jessie Rankin who pretty much did whatever he saw the pastor do grabbed a spatula from one of the serving tables and played a make believe bass. The utensil had sauce on it that dripped all on his clothes. Jessie didn't care, in fact he just laughed and keep pretend playing anyway. Sister Bergen, who was helping with the food serving, shook her head putting her hands on her hips. She would normally have scolded, but she just started to laugh before skipping in step.

Barbeque chicken, ribs, turkey legs, hamburgers and Sister Mia Conner's favorite smell—sautéed onions had arrested the air. The savory aroma traveling for almost a half mile from Cedar Brook Park where Family Life Church was having its Glorifest—its annual, meet the community and family outing day. The Park was just several blocks from the church building. It had more shade, green grass, and other amenities than the church parking lot. Strategically, it was still close enough for the visitors to connect the community outreach with FLC.

Everyone was fellowshipping. Some of the guys were tossing around the football trying a little informal game of hand touch, with trees, boxes, and hats as the goals. Rodney Williams was hired as the DJ. He played the music for Sunday mornings worship and other special events when asked and his full-time job permitted.

It was around six in the evening, on this second Saturday in July. Still early for summer, night not arriving until around eight. Usually the community, and those parishioner—who usually never stayed longer than they had to after church, would have been gone. But not this year, people were still walking over, and gathering at the stage.

Jason and some of the other kids had their ear phones on listening to their cell phone's playlist.

"Put on some Kirk," someone screamed referring to gospel artist *Kirk Franklin.*

"Put on some *Mary Mary*, "screamed someone else, coming from the direction of grandmother—Sister Ida Nelson.

Rodney looked around. Others people were in to their conversations Deacon Frank was still eating—potato salad and cake and a couple spoonfuls of ambrosia. Rodney started with *Martha Munezzi.*

A couple of people stood up and began clapping their hands. Others stood and began swaying and lightly stepping to the music. Angela Murray was the event coordinator. She grabbed the mike and encouraged the audience to do one of the slides. Soon everyone was up. Rodney played one gospel tune after another.

Nobody saw me at first. I was in the crowds on the floor. I enjoyed it. I loved to dance. And I tried to dance with everyone who was up.

Five songs had played, when the Holy Spirit set in. Everybody at Family Life was laughing, full of joy, and praising God for something he had done in their life. Some were rejoicing for a miraculous triumph over a situation. Others were jubilant because of a physical healing. Others were dancing because of a financial breakthrough and a heaven sent increase. Still others rejoiced for restoration in relationships. Some were exuberant in remembrance of a victory or something they had overcome.

Second year members Katie and Vince Nichols were dancing with their little daughter—Jessica, born with a hole in her heart. The doctor said she wouldn't make it to six months. The little reddish blonde haired girl was now two. Her mother was pregnant with her little brother. Minister Ralph, in a wheelchair, who hadn't walked in months, stood up and shuffled his way, towards the stage, through the crowd. He stopped half way to do a jig. The place exploded in praise.

Circle dances in groups of eight—more or less—were formed all over the grounds. Several people were doing the holy dance. Some of the sisters were trying to hold them as if they were flying away. Pastor Clarence said just let them go. They're dancing with the Holy Spirit. Everyone was up moving in some kind of way. Minister Jerry, who Pastor Clarence often referred to as prophet, walked up to the DJ—and motioned for the mike.

"Praise God in the dance. Praise Him for his goodness and mercy. Let them sing praises unto him with the timbrel and harp... For the Lord takes pleasure in his people. Let the saints be joyful in glory. Let them sing aloud upon their beds. Let the high praises of God be in their mouth."

He was quoting from Psalms 149, at least his Holy Spirit excited version—all there, but not necessarily, in order.

Donjae wished she had stayed quietly in the bathroom stall anonymous to the criticism. No one would have known then. Two hours later, she found herself exposed at a gay bar. She wasn't gay, but the temptation to have fun and be accepted overcame her.

Preefies wasn't really a gay bar by name. It was where a lot of younger adult experimenting hung out. The representation was accurate and the unofficially name would apply at least by eighty percent of the crowd. Still most of the patron started coming out of curiosity.

"There's an empty table, pointed Tiara, acknowledging a table across the darkened main room. Blue and red streams of lights, from the ceiling of metal rafters, broke in and out of the fake fog blown from the vents at the edge of the dance floor. The three girls ignored both the swarm of dancers in the center and the human shadows at the tables and headed toward their claimed seats before someone else grabbed it.

"What are you drinking? A waitress with bright orange short hair had unknowingly followed them to their table. "If it's anything other the soda then I have to see ID."

"I'm good," Ravine answered first.

"You have to order something," responded the waitress. Her voice slightly raised adjusting to the new beat that had just mixed in. "To stay you have to order something."

"Okay bring me a Coke. How much is that any way."

"Three dollars"

"What? Oh well."

"I'll have a beer," chimed in Donjae

"Beer! Didn't you just come from church girl," questioned Ravine, rolling her eyes, at the same time, her mouth wide open. Who would have thought?"

"It's just a beer," confirmed Tiara. "Enjoy your beer girl."

"And you," asked the waitress, now looking at Tiara.

"Apple martini... yes an apple martini."

"Oh Lord... I guess I'm driving. Y'all better not let me get stuck in this place."

"Like I said, anything other than soda or water or juice, I need ID."

Donjae and Tiara both dug into their handbags and retrieved their license.

"Okay we been here a half hour. What now?" checked Ravine, resting her face into her hands and arms propped on the table.

"You want to dance?" Donjae whispered, but sounding loud enough over the music for the other two to hear.

"Together? " Ravine stared crossed eyed at Donjae.

"You do know where we are," reminded the new girl.

"Yeah, but I ain't no lesbian," pushed back Ravine.

"Well neither am I.... not that I..."

"Not that you what." Ravine interrupted, not giving the new girl a chance to reveal if her statement was just an attempt to be politically correct or if it was her behavior. "Are you...."

"I mean, I don't think I am." answered Donjae, speaking her thoughts, attempting to be transparent with her new companions. "It's just that I feel comfortable more so with girls than always trying to put out a conversation with boys. It seems like I always have to be on the offense or defense with guys, with girls, most girls, I can be myself."

"I know what you mean," interjected Tiara, "but that don't mean you're gay. It just means you're not ready for boys yet."

"Should we be having this conversation here?" laughed Ravine, taking a sip of her Coke. "Come on let's all just get up and dance together. Since we're here let's have some fun."

Donjae was already up, and heading towards the floor, looking back at Tiara, and beckoning to her with her right hand. Tiara swallowed the rest of her martini not wanting to leave her drink unattended. She reached her hand back to her best friend. Ravine pulled the cord tighter on her hand bag before placing her hand in Tiara's, pulling her whole body up. The two headed towards the floor following Donjae.

"I think somebody just rubbed my butt," said Ravine. Jerking her behind forward and looking around hoping not to see anyone. She didn't. "Time to go."

"Did you like it," said Tiara laughing. "Was it like cherry lipstick?"

"That's not funny. Time to go," responded Ravine.

Donjae wasn't laughing or smiling. She was still thinking about what she said earlier. She smiled at Tiara. "Whatever you want to do"

"Girls," announced Tiara, already moving, stepping, bending her legs, hands over her head circling her hands like waving a flag, "This isn't *ClubK4C*."

"What's that?" Ask Ravine. The music seemed to get louder. All three girls were moving now. Moving more so in time with the crowd, on the floor than the music.

"It's a kid's club—Christian—has a big lion" answered Ravine smiling.

"Cool," said Donjae, "We have to go there sometime."

"You crazy, girl," said Tiara.

"Dancing is fun but it's also other things. We sing the song when the Spirit of the Lord is up on me I will dance like David danced. It's true. There's a spirit behind dancing. In Isaiah 61:3 God told His people he gives us the garment of praise for the spirit of heaviness. Some of the words for praise means to dance. It's a spiritual thing. It operates greater than in just a physical world." It was Pastor Clarence Sunday to preach.

"There's a spirit behind it. And, it can get on you. Now I'm not saying it's wrong to do the *Electric Slide* or the *Cupid Shuffle*. Those are social type dancing. But when you dance and get into it, you become connected with the music, and the place, and whatever is in the music, and in the club, could get on you.

We all like to have fun sometimes. We had fun at the church outing. We did the Slide. We did the Shuffle. Well I didn't, but some of y'all did. But when we started to praise God, and rejoice, and dance, because of who he is, and what he did, standing on his word, his spirit—the Holy Spirit came on us. He came not from the place of the music, although most of the music was anointed, but his glory came from within him, and from him within us. And, yes, he was there. And you know what, the Bible says, Jesus will praise dance in the midst of a worshipping congregation."

7

Rita's Dance

Here We Go

Then Miriam the prophet, Aaron's sister, took a tambourine and led all the women as they played their tambourines and danced. [21] And Miriam sang this song: "Sing to the LORD, for he has triumphed gloriously; he has hurled both horse and rider into the sea."—Exodus 15:20, 21NLT

Miriam watched her baby brother in the Nile River making sure that the crocodiles didn't find him before Pharaoh's daughter did. The plan went better than expected. God's plans always did. The childless Egyptian royalty found her son. Perhaps, first thought given by her god Rah—the sun god. It was later she'd understand, Yah—who made the sun, moon, stars and she herself, was in control.

The miraculous baby had to eat. Miriam came out of hiding as the princess sought a nurse maid. "I know someone," said Miriam. At Bithiah's approval, she brought to her Moses's mother—Jochebed to nurse the destined prophet.

"I will call him "Mosheh," in Hebrew it means to "draw out", decided the new mother, because she drew him out the water. "Moses" (how the others would call him) calling would grow in Egypt, though only preparing him for his born assignment. He was called to deliver his people, slaves to Pharaoh, out of four hundred years of bondage, building that which would never be their own.

God met Moses in the wilderness. An angel appeared, in the form of a bush that burned but was not consumed. This Holy God declared to him his name, sending him back to where he had come, to break the news to the king of Egypt. "Let my people go"

Pharaoh was stubborn and Yahweh would visit with horrible plagues designed two-fold. He silenced the pride of his people's enemy. Secondly, his people would know and see, he was their all-powerful deliverer that none could successfully oppose. Pharaoh resilience to be hardhearted ended when the death angel visited killing all the first born, including Pharaoh's son. Israel would be saved by a sacrifice, their obedience, and faith. It was the first Passover. God delivered his people by protecting them with blood.

Finally, Pharaoh relinquished his hold and freed Israel. The change of heart was temporary. As they left the land of captivity, the enemy soon pursued, trapping them at the Red Sea with nowhere to go but through. And through, they went.

"Stretch your staff over the water," instructed God to Moses. He did. The sea departed and Israel went across on dry land. Pharaoh pursued again, only this time, Israel enemies would bother them no more. In the morning light Israel looked out upon a now quiet and horizontal sea. They did not see any trace of their enemy.

Before the thoughts could surface. "They turned around. Perhaps it wasn't really them. Perhaps just our fear getting the best of us." Or, before they could forget in the moment—the deliverance of God. Miriam, now a prophetess, beckon by the Spirit, grabbed a tambourine and gathered the women—young and old. She began to dance. The others followed. She sang a song. In praise, sealed in history—the fate of the enemy and God's stamp of deliverance.

"Well Miss Rita, here we go. Lord help me."

She was waiting for the emcee to announce her. It wasn't the first time the divorced, thirty-three years old mom had said that. Many times over the years that included her finishing college, marrying Calvin, and doing everything in order like she was supposed to. She even kept herself holy until marriage. At least if you didn't count the one time with Barry, in the car, at the park. They didn't do anything, but enough went on to make her think about it for a long time. Barry could have been the one too. She really liked him, but they were young. She was leaving for school. He was staying at home with high dreams of entrepreneurship.

In college, she met Calvin Richardson. They started to date. Her one summer back at home and connecting with Barry was only to find he was engaged. She never came back home after that.

"Well Miss Rita here we go."

She washed her hands, sucked in some air, and forced a smile. It wasn't that she wasn't happy being pregnant, but the onset of new experiences always made her nervous at first. She would resolve, but she had to get through her moment which sometimes took days. Calvin adjusted himself on the couch, when he saw his cute, sleepy-eyed, love coming into the room. He was a little bored with what was on TV and her entrance seemed to bring a shift in his mood.

"Are you ready?" smiled Rita.

"Ready for what?" said Calvin, looking up at his wife.

"I believe I'm pregnant."

Calvin adjusted himself fully up on the couch. He was slouching, but now full seated.

"You mean? How? I mean"

Rita rolled her eyes she knew her husband was choked. "Well I'm sure you know how," said the registered nurse. "If the 'test in the box' is accurate? I am. I still would like to see my doctor to confirm."

"But those things are pretty accurate," smiled Calvin. His voice raised in intensity. The central air conditioner fan kicked on at that moment the draft caught Rita's perfume and carried it right to Calvin nose further tripping his emotions.

"Yeah, they are, so as of right now, we're pregnant, as they say. I sure wish that were true. I don't know who came up with that phrase."

Calvin was up from the couch. Squeezing his wife. Her fragrance totally over riding anything else in the room and in his heart. "You know I am with you through all this girl. Anything you need. I am there hand and foot."

And he was. The bump in the road was the knock at the door six months later. The doorbell rang followed by a several knocks. Peering first through the keyhole, Rita open the door. She was home. It was her day off. Calvin was at work. A little girl selling Girl Scout cookies with her mom, she supposed, deduced first from what she saw through the little lens.

"Yes?"

"Is this the Richardson residence?" Quickly asked the brown skinned women with a blue blazer and blue skirt, who now looked, to Rita, like a social worker.

"Yes?"

"Does Calvin Richardson... Vinnie... live here."

The nickname shook Rita. No one called Calvin that in years.

"Yes... may I ask... who, why you're asking? Who are you?"

"My name's Jacklyn Stevenson," answered the woman. "This pretty young girl is Crystal."

"Hi Crystal," Interrupted Rita with a quick smile, not forced like normal, easy because the little girl was cute and well poised.

"I am Crystal's aunt. Her mother name is Beatrice. Beatrice Stevenson."

"Are you selling something, running for something... soccer fundraiser? I don't have any money on me if you are," inquired Rita. Redness was flushing her French latte complexion. Mentally, she was trying to override silly thoughts that were trying to surface.

"No, nothing like that I probably should be talking to Calvin. I mean Mr. Richardson.

"Why? How do you know my husband?" Rita's voice now more pointed.

"Well I knew him briefly. It's my sister Bea that knew him more."

"Well Calvin, my husband, is at the church right now in his office. He's a pastor."

"Oh, Mrs. Richardson, I am so sorry," said the woman. The little girl looked up at her aunt without moving her head. "Can I go to the church or can we come back when your husband is home?"

Rita was massaging her baby bump. She hadn't really done that much this far into the pregnancy, but instinctively she was doing it now, as if comforting her new born from some pending danger. "Well you can go to the church. His secretary may let you see him depending on his appointments. But do you mind telling me the relationship between my husband, you, your sister, and the young girl."

"Mrs. Richardson" whispering "I have reason to believe Crystal is your husband's daughter."

The proverbial knock at the door. The child looking for their daddy was so. Calvin really didn't know he had a child. He wasn't always a preacher. A Christian, but with some wild days. Beatrice was a girl he dated in high school.

"Only one time Rita." He swallowed hard turning and looking purposely into his wife eyes, hoping she would see into him that he was telling the truth. "Only one time, we did it. And that was when I was leaving for college. It was kind of like us saying good bye to each other.

I heard she was pregnant. But, I thought. Well, my ignorance and indiscretion. But I don't blame Bea. If I had a known, I'd..." He was cautious how he continued. It may have meant not meeting Rita.

Beatrice had a drug addiction. A dirty needle. She was dying from aides. Her sister, a sales representative, her only living relative, was always on the road. Now, there were three children the Richardson's had to raise. Rita and Calvin had their first baby, and then another three years later.

Unfortunately, Pastor Calvin never fully overcame what he called an indiscretion. According to the book you really shouldn't council women alone, especially one's having marital problems. He said he loved her, the new girl, and although he didn't what to hurt Rita and his kids, he left her and the church. The divorce was hard. Not from a legal stand point, but spiritually and emotionally.

Crystal was now twenty. She stayed with the woman who raised her from the tweens. Dancing was a way to bring together the spiritual and the emotional. Rita had forgiven Calvin, but the pain surfaced many times.

She watched a woman she had admired from a workshop she attended—Candace Bryant. God spoke to Rita through her lips. Then afterward Candace danced. Rita never saw praise dance before. They didn't have it at *First John's AME Church* that she attended. She took some classes at nearby *Riverside Pentecostal* and she loved it. Pastor Ida McKenzie approved. Although no dance ministry was started in the church, Rita danced at certain services with pastor's approval. The East Coast Liturgical Dance Recital was her first event outside of her church. Her pastor actually gave her the flyer invitation.

I knew Rita would do well. Every time she danced she was letting more and more go. Enemies of her mind that kept trying to pull her back into bondage. When she danced she could see the freedom.

"Okay Rita you can do this," speaking to herself aloud.

It was a duet dance, mother and daughter. Her partner echoed. "Yes, mom we can"

8

Ginger's Dance

The Place on Stage

Ginger Teris Robinson swung her long auburn hair to her right side, behind her shoulder, with one quick flip of her head. Her slender frame was carved and chiseled, five foot nine standing upright, tall and poised. When she walked, one foot, crossed in line, in front of the other unintentionally causing her full figured behind to twitch fluidly. Her apricot cream skin made her look Caucasian in certain lighting but her full, persimmon, lips especially when glossed, revealed her blended African American ancestry. Closer up, her eye color was the envy of other women, nicknaming her Hazel. Others understood why her mother named her Ginger.

The twenty-six-year-old was beautiful and she presented herself that way. She never considered herself a diva, being beautiful was deeper in her. Even when she wasn't trying to gain attention, Ginger carried herself with a sexiness that made most men turn, daring some to take the forbidden second look. Ginger T, was the name she thought about using if she ever went secular with her dancing. It was just a thought, ditching it after she realized it sounded it too much like a stripper. Some of her friends called her that any way. When they did, it still sounded stagey, but swank.

She stretched her long arms again, hands clasped, high, full length over her head, unlocking fingers, before slowly lowering them to her side, still poised. Grabbing her duffle, and slinging it over her other shoulder, she picked up her half full bottle of *Pure Life* spring water, and headed to the greenroom.

The competition was important to her, but in some regards, just another recital. This was her twentieth. Twenty-first, if you consider the one in her home town ten years ago. It was an outside event and it rained. She vowed never to do an outside event again unless it was for Hollywood.

It was Friday night Ginger dabbed Chalet on her neck smiled in the mirror. The clock posted 9 pm but she didn't look. She grabbed her cell phone, keys and headed out the bedroom, to the door.

"Where you going?" asked Diamond, her friend and mentee.

"Misties," responded Ginger.

"Don't you have to dance tomorrow?" asked again Diamond, knowing Ginger, yet still a little surprised, knowing how big this recital was.

"I'm just going to be a few hours. I'm hooking up with Reevie. Where just going to hang out. I'm just going for something to do."

"Something to do, you got to dance at the recital tomorrow. Shouldn't you be resting or praying. I know you probably don't need the practice. You got that."

"Yeah I got that." Snapped Ginger sarcastically, trying to mimic confidence. "I prayed about it already. I practiced today. What more is there to do? I might well have some fun. You know what I mean?"

And that's what she normally did. She was still a good girl. She danced, but mostly she entertained herself by finding creative ways to turn guys downs that approached her. Ginger didn't really have to flirt, men just came on to her like that.

Although disguised, she was still hoping for Mr. Right. She assured herself she would know him when the moment came. Deep inside, she toyed with the ideal that the man she would marry would be a preacher like her father.

"Alright," sighed Diamond, knowing that when Ginger's mind was fixed there was no changing her. The only one that could do that was her father and that was with reluctance. She said goodnight to her roommate as she headed out the door.

Ginger met Diamond two years ago, and the two young women became friends, although not instantly. Their friendship was thrown together. Diamond was sixteen. They met at a program in Philadelphia. It wasn't really a recital. It was a church program, mostly liturgical dance, maybe one solo singer performance, and a skit.

Diamond's presence took the stage and she danced in worship. She was good, her steps on point. And, she flowed in the music. Ginger was impressed. She never told anyone, but despite her years of training, she could see in Diamond true liberty. She wanted that but didn't know how to step over into it. They talked afterwards and complemented each other.

When Ginger danced, Diamond saw in her a command of the stage and song. Ginger's approaching to dancing was always a 'matter-of-fact'. She just thought, this gift, it belongs to God. Let me give it to him now. In her sauciness, she had actually touched into an element of true ministry. The dance was supposed be for him and the people should receive it that way. Although a schooled dancer, having the years of training, on the floor she never followed a regimen. She practiced, but let the Spirit guide her steps and use what she had studied.

Their friendship was kindled. Diamond looked up to Ginger. She loved her personality and respected her as being the oldest. She was like a sister. As a friend, she was able to talk to Ginger about other things as well. She didn't know but Ginger found some stability in her as well.

The previous dancer had just finished. The audience was still praising and worship God. Ginger could sense God's presence and she waited back stage for the curtain. Her dance started in position center stage. The audience was still in worship. The DJ played the end of the song again—*Yes*, by *Shekinah Glory*. Ginger loved the song as well, but always thought the ten-minute piece was just too long for a recital.

"Okay Lord, I'm ready, use me." She thought the prayer. She knew God heard her. There were times she just tried to find words she believed were right. Sometimes she'd copy her father's prayers. The ones she heard him say before he ministered behind the pulpit, or when he sang.

"Now y'all bettah clap when I'm out there," smiled Ginger. She was serious. She used to say that because she wanted the approval from the audience to bring her confirmation. Now she prayed it because she believed it brought glory to God. In other words, the people got it. The applauses, the hands raised, and the occasional shout-outs were confirmation that they got it. Nevertheless, she had learned that if they didn't, it was okay.

Mr. Charles loved it when Ginger danced. He knew ministry and sensed the spirit, but he loved it when the skill was there. He believed, God could use—all of that, even when others his age thought it didn't take—all of that, to minister for the Lord.

He had a closer connection with Ginger. He was there in the delivery room, with her mother, his wife the day she was born. She was his youngest and his princess.

There was something with Ginger although she struggled in holiness at times, the Spirit would use her immensely. When she was at the club, she was there having her fun. When she danced, she gave it all to the Lord, never holding back, intrinsically finding her love more, every time, in every song and with every step.

Princess Hadassah stood before King Artaxerxes. She was gorgeous. Her pearl turquoise gown draping her slender body and almond tan skin. Long black hair crowned on her head and dropped down, joining with her garment, in thick strands but as were brushed to silkiness a thousand times. She wore her crown. Frankincense, spice, and wild flowers of Lebanon blended to fill the room—the king's room with a trance of ecstasy. Many times before, she stood before the king. Usually all in response to his call. Tonight was different. It was her desire to see her love.

Esther, as the records of Ancient Persia would name her, was a woman chosen and set in time. A slave girl in the beginning in this strange land. One of the beautiful females taken from their families at the request of the conquering kingdom. The king's wife had disobeyed him and she was exiled as according to decree. Therefore, stopping a rebellion of woman towards their men.

The King needed another wife and so the pageant was launched. The young Benjaminite girl was taken along with the collection, sought to join the king's harem, with the potential of being his new queen. The disparity, either be a slave girl or be exalted in royalty. God favored Hadassah and she became Artaxerxes bride. Hadassah didn't know that it would be her beauty, poise, and position that would save her people from annihilation.

It was illegal according to Persian law for the queen to enter the king's court without being summoned. However, the king smiled in delight at Esther's presence and called his love to him. In her humility, granted her request.

9
Diamond's Dance

All of Me

Diamond, Honey, are you up? You got twenty minutes to shower and dress—less time to eat. I'll put a *Nutri Bar* out for you. There a glass of juice also. If you got time eat some of your father's oatmeal. I'll make him some more when he gets back in from his walk.

Diamond smiled and pulled the blanket up to her ears. "Momma is so good to me, Daddy too," she thought. She drifted for a moment. She thought about school, her friends, the basketball game today in gym, the algebra test, the party, and Bobby Miles. She smiled again, yawned, stretched lifting the cover off herself and sat up on the mattress.

"I guess I am up now", almost speaking her thoughts, surveying the room before starting her regimen. Diamond knew when she got up it would be all routine and she didn't mind. It was what she was used too. Mom and dad were staunch with their discipline. It was almost as if they bred her that way, because she couldn't seem to function without some type of routine.

Michael despised David. Her husband the king dancing before the maidens in the street. She looked over the balcony, three stories down. David had come out of his clothes. Close enough, King David stripped down to his loin cloth, before adorning a side-less apron called and ephod.

The crowds followed. The priest, along with the pole bearers of the ark, followed carrying the golden box, with the kneeled cherubim. The musicians followed to the sides. Trumpeters charged the air. All around, it was like a thousand cymbals and tambourines being beat in symphony. The streets of Israel had erupted in joy. At the same time, there was solemnity in the air like the quiet before a storm. An expectancy that had not been felt in Israel for long time. People and king, assured the presence of God had returned.

David had tried before to bring it back, but the wrong way. Uzzah was killed by the same glory of God they sought. Something had gone array. There was a right and wrong way to usher in the Shekinah presence of God. He found the book and instructed the priest. Convinced that with gladness and joy, this instrument of God's presence, be brought back. The king would dance, stopping every six paces to sacrifice.

The ark had blessed Obededom's house where it stayed for three months. It had destroyed the idol—Dagon of the Philistines who had stolen it. These pagans suffered hemorrhoids because of it. So, as David danced shamelessly that day in Israel in the streets. He did not care. He did not care if the elders disapproved him, or if the young girls stared, or the men laughed, or his own wife despised him. The presence of Yahweh was back in the camp, with all his might, presence, and favor. "It's before the Lord," said the king. "It's before the Lord."

"You should go to the party," pressed Leeza. The dreamy-eyed cheerleader looked at Diamond and smiled. The locker room was almost empty. A couple other girls' voices, on the parallel row, could be faintly heard, with the zippering of gym bags. Steam from the showers hadn't completely dissipated, making the gray and pink room humid, and smelling like warm skin.

"Why, there's nothing there for me," responded Diamond, sitting on the bench, bending over her knees, towards the floor, to pull on her shoe.

"Well, all the kids will be there. Ones like us—smart, athletic, and have some direction in life."

"Yeah, that's okay, but that's still not the type of environment that I need to be in. I don't drink, smoke or anything..."

"...Or anything... that's what I mean Di," interrupted Leeza. "You gotta have some fun. You'll be graduating in a year from high school and you never had a date. You never had boyfriend. You never had a kiss. You never had..."

"...And I never will," blurted Diamond. It was her turn to interrupt. Now standing, pulling her mixed purple, nylon, skirt up to waist, looking down making sure it wasn't too high over her knees. "Not until I'm ready."

"Girl don't you ever think about any of it?"

She hadn't so much thought about the last thing that Leeza hinted. And definitely not a boyfriend, to have to answer to, but a kiss and a male friend to talked too, was something she thought about.

"Well..."

"I know you do," said Leeza, answering the question for her classmate and zipping up her jeans at the same time.

"I'm just trying to stay focused. I got goals."

"We all do girl... but a little fun sometimes."

"Yeah, I know."

"Hey, Bobby's going to be there," posted Leeza, hoping this play would coach Diamond's desire.

"So..."

"Don't say it like that. I know you like him. Who don't like the basketball players anyway? Tall dark and handsome."

"Yeah he is cute." Diamond smiled, this time out of one side of her mouth, hoping Leeza would see her interest, proving in her some normalcy.

"So, you're coming tonight?" asked the cheerleader captain, tugging at the bottom of her number eleven Philadelphia Eagles' jersey, she just slipped over her head.

"I didn't say that. And besides you know how protective my parents are. My dad will ask a million questions. Starting with are these kids Christians?"

"Well just tell him you going with me. I'm a Christian," said Leeza, not even blinking.

"Oh now, you want me to lie?"

"Ha funny. I do go to church," said Leeza. The two were now standing looking in the fog cleared locker room mirror.

"But that doesn't make you a Christian." Diamond was quick to respond with conviction. It was a reality she heard and learned many times in her life.

"Okay... look call your folks," replied Leeza, deliberately not debating her church going friend. Also not really believing what she said was that important. "Say you going to be hanging with me. We're going to eat at my house and were going to see a movie."

"So you do want me to lie to my folks?"

"No we can plan to do that and then our plans may get interrupted."

It wasn't a total lie. They did eat dinner at Leeza's. Lasagna and cabbage. It was an interesting combo. But it was very good. Mrs. Smith was a great cook.

"Mom we're going to the movies. It's a late one so don't wait up."

The party was in full swing when they arrived. It was *Fizzies*—a teen club down town. The place was dark and the music was loud. When the door opened the atmosphere hit Diamond strong. It was like walking into another dimension.

Bobby wasn't there, but Kevin was. Kevin Stanstill was from Harrington, another city, and another school.

"He's fine," she thought, trying not to stare, noticing him first, as if he was the only guy in the place. It was mutual, as soon as Diamond came through the door, she had Kevin's attention.

"Hey I'm Kevin. Do you want to dance?" Kevin was in her face already. She smelled apples.

"You want some," holding up a white pen like apparatus to about eye level. He was smoking one of those electric cigarettes that you fill with flavored tobacco juice.

"No thanks, I'll dance though."

Although she felt out of place. Dancing was her one thing. With it, she could fit in anywhere. The music was a little techno, but she could flow. Praise dancing wasn't all she knew. Diamond practiced everything—tap, jazz, ballet, hip hop, waltz. Last time she waltzed was with her daddy at the *Father Daughter Ball* hosted by the church. She began, left foot, right foot, back and forth. She started twisting her hips slightly, then raising her hands in the air, and then she was gone. Kevin couldn't keep up. She found herself dancing with all the guys on the floor, just having fun.

Leeza was clapping, as well as others from school that she knew. The whole place was clapping, including people she didn't know, from elsewhere. When the next song came on she stayed on the floor. It hit her. Her dancing moved up into her body and she began to flaunt. She could feel the sensuality rise up in her. It scared her for a moment. She didn't know where this was going.

"Oh God, what am doing?" It hit her again, but this time it wasn't the feel of her flesh. The lasagna and cabbage Leeza mother had cooked, turned another deep physical feeling in her. The room became blurry. She felt dizzy. She cupped her hands over her mouth, caught a glimpse of the lady's room and ran towards it. Barely, she made it. Couldn't make the toilet, but vomited into the sink.

Although it felt good, the parmesan and greens broke the desire to go back to the floor that night and for a long time. But the taste remained and what was outside of her church life stuck in her heart.

"I hear you got some moves," smiled Bobby, almost running to catch up with Diamond. Her athletic legs put her almost at a jog pace even when she was strolling from class.

She hid the smile and responded. "You talking to me?"

"Yes," said Bobby. "Moves, I hear you got some moves. You're a dancer."

"I am a dancer. A liturgical dancer."

"What's that?" Questioned Bobby.

"I guess you say, I dance for Jesus."

"Dance for Jesus. How and where you do that?" Bobby was interested, but more so, how he could know the pretty junior better. He had a goal in mind. He momentarily forgot that what he was told didn't sound like a Jesus dance.

"I dance in church. You never heard of praise dancing?" asked Diamond slowing her pace a little to allow more time to talk to her crush.

"Yeah, yeah, I heard of it but never really seen it. I would like too though. I mean, I would like to see you do it." He didn't really care about the church part, but he was on the roll. He was convinced that if he just got pass that he could score with his new interest.

I was at Diamond's church the day that Bobby came. It was the third Sunday, the day that Pastor Reeves allowed the dance team to minister. It wasn't my desire for them to meet, at least not then. Five years later it may have been better after Diamond graduated college and got her life on track. By then, Bobby would have detoxed from the lust he was addicted to and seriously think about his life. His dream was to be a counselor that specialized with helping the marriages of rich athletes. Of course, after he got beyond the dream of being a basketball star. A great man of God, super-fun father, and a loving husband is what I could see in him. I had a long talk with Bobby that Sunday. I had a long talked with Diamond as well.

10
Reevie

Beauty is Vain

"I can dance Ginger. I don't know about doing the church thing again, but I can dance."

"You should try it, "encouraged Ginger, "maybe that's what God has for you."

"I guess. You know I want to do something...sing, act. Daddy wants me to go to law school. Ever since I won that mock trial case, in high school History, he sees me as some female attorney from *Law & Order*. All daddy sees is his little girl. He didn't know that five of the boys on the jury wanted to date me. He doesn't see the judge would just let me win no matter what I said. They love me. I'm smart but I'll use everything God has given me to win."

"Girl you're something else," pronounced Ginger with a twinge of distaste. Normally, Reevie wasn't the type of person she'd hang out with. Ginger preferred being with people who just liked to chill and get silly now and then. Not egotistical people, like Reevie, admittedly, who was entertained by the attention she got because of her looks.

Both young women were beautiful. The difference, Ginger didn't hang it out there to dry. Her looks just made her more confident in herself. And, if she wasn't attractive, she'd still do what she did, but would just find something else upon which to base her confidence. She did know inexcusably that guys found her alluring. So she sometimes used that reality to have some fun.

The two connected when they found out, they had common relatives. They weren't sure if this was by blood or just association. They thought they might be cousins, although neither of them took the time to really check it out.

"You did the flags before at your old church. What happened?" Ginger questioned Reevie, while having lunch at *Whompers*. The local fast food joint had the best burgers anywhere. It was Tuesday's lunch meeting, both women's day to cheat on their diets.

"I guess I got tired of it," answered Reevie, pulling a pickle out of the side of her sandwich and then inserting back in under the top bun. "I mean, I don't know if I was into it. I thought I felt something. I felt like I was doing something for God."

"So why did you stop."

"They stopped me. They said I was causing distraction. Crazy. Probably their fault. Those old deacons you know. Smiling. I know what they're thinking." The auburn haired, brown eyed, woman sipped her vanilla milkshake and continued. "Up to then, I really never saw myself that way before. Gee, I was only thirteen when I did the flags."

"Did you do them right?" asked Ginger.

"Well I think, that was the other thing, Miss Carol didn't ever take us to one of those retreats or a class. You know. There's always more to learn."

Craig Pierce ducked, exaggerating a little bit this time. The first time, he hid his expectation, and slid over in the seat, closer to Maggie Westbrook, who he didn't know, and waited for the moment to pass. He didn't want to get hit any more. The one church sister—dancer, with the flag, hit him once already, tapping the top of his head with the pole. It didn't hurt, but he could still feel, where the connection was made. No one else saw it, but the usher standing almost right in back of him. She stepped back several feet when the flag ministry team came down the aisle. Laughing inwardly, she laid her hand on Craig's, a visitor at the church, shoulder. "Got you, didn't she?"

Craig brushed it off by nodding his head and smiling. Flags were everywhere. Huge colorful flags and long banners, on six foot poles, some as if filling the room, with every swing, by the all-female team. Milestone Methodist Church added flags to their liturgical dance ministry and now almost every Sunday the bold and majestic colors flapped and waved expectedly at almost every worship service.

Pastor Delores Crosby and Reta Wilson saw flags at a worship gathering a few years back. Reta, head of *Milestone's Dance Ministry*, loved it. She immediately connected to the worship. Pastor Crosby was motivated by churches from different denominations coming together and worshipping, with each sharing in their approach into God's presence.

"Hallelujah, You are worthy. King of kings and Lord of Lord"

Holy music filled the air. The drummer, the guitarist, and the keyboardist were entranced. There was unity in the rhythm that extended beyond the instruments.

One of the churches, who were presenting with flags, had brochures on their display table about an upcoming dance retreat. One of the training session was on using flags in worship.

Pastor Delores, with very little convincing, agreed to send Minister Wilson along with others on the team to the conference in the Fall. The pastor's ideal was to bring it back to the church. She made it known, "If we're going to implement flags into our worship, we need to do it right."

Carol Delaney went to the same conference that Reta Wilson went too. She was convinced, "You can't really find it in scripture. It's more so to give the women and girls something to do."

Carol was her pastor's right hand person. If the five-hundred-member church would have had elders or some other confirming title, she would have had it. It was okay, she and the pastor knew her role. "Okay, dancing is in there (referring to biblical liturgy), but flags," questioned the forty-seven year old church elder, resolving to keep an open mind.

"His banner over me is love," quoted Dr. Perot, a key note at the conference, from Songs of Solomon 2:4. She was making sense with her theology on worship and the use of flags. "One of God's names is Jehovah Nissi the 'Lord is my Victory or my Banner'. When we wave flags, we remind ourselves of who he is in our lives. "

The Abiding Presence Chapel main auditorium held about 2000 comfortably. It was packed. Dance ministry from all over the country and parts of the world had come to learn more about worship and dance ministry. The room was as speckled with color of faces as it was with facets of denominations and levels of worship. Yet undeniably, everyone in attendance had a desire to grow in their discipline.

"Flags also represent the victory of a kingdom or a team. They serve as a collective voice declaring a standard. Like saluting the United States flag, it's not the flag, but what it stands for. Flags also express unity in the nations," continued the five foot six middle aged woman, with black hair toned with strings of gray. Waving her arms and hands back and forth over her head, she emphasized the point. "In the Olympics, all the flags raised, from all the nations, coming together, representing people from all nations, together in unity.

The banners we raise also represent, in Christ, people from every nation and tongue washed in the blood of the Lamb. It reminds us of the worship in Heaven, in Revelations chapter five. And please remember, flag ministry is not an incantation to conjure up the Holy Spirit. God has always moved by faith, and faith in his Word."

It wasn't the demonstration and training at the event but the Word of God that connected with Carol. She tried to put it together, when she got back to the church. The dancing was okay, much better than before some years ago when they started dance ministry as part of women's outreach ministry which extended to all ages.

The pastor was concerned about the girls not being challenged. Some of the girl who joined the dance team were single mothers who would come into the church looking for help, in some cases, but then drop off after they got back on their feet. Others dancers were girls who their parents kept them in church. These girls would use the ministry as a transition place to bridge the time before exiting to college, away from church, parents, and pastors. Dance ministry allowed them to temporarily break the monotonous routine of the Sunday society and give church a little soul, rock, and hip hop.

The older women, would faithfully participate, but there was no measure of spiritual growth. All in all, dance ministry presented more opportunity, in most churches, for women to minister in the service. Before the nineties, singing in the choir was of the few pulpits for females Christians to openly share their worship. Whereas, it was not as much, men danced too. Interpretive Dance, as it was also called, was sometimes expressed as God ministering through the Arts. It was still mostly woman and girls getting involved. Contrarily, Carol's pastor didn't really see it, at first, as a strong church service ministry. She envisioned it more so as a club that could be used to engage the ladies of the church. So, to some of the women of *United Baptist*, it was the opportunity to do something.

Reevie Phillips was only fourteen, the church was next door, several houses down from hers. She would go. There was something about it that attracted her. She loved the music. She loved the quietness that existed even in the midst of the sometimes loud music and preaching. It was like being close to God, at least that what she got from it. Friday night is when the women and the girls gathered in the church community hall—to talk, be social, to turn the music up and dance.

"It's a mess," said Sister Tonya Evans to Laura Murphy. The girls weren't really following any known instructions. And some of the dancing was questionable from a liturgical standing. The young girls thought it was a way just to be free, while using Christian music and the sanction of the church to do it.

"No harm done," responded the thirty-year-old Sister Murphy, "they're just girls. Better to have them shake it to *Hezekiah Walker* than

Cardi B or *Beyoncé*. And as long as they don't start twerking." Some of the girls were close.

Reevie came one of the Fridays. In fact, it was my idea. I talked to her one day on the street. She tried to ignore me at first. Mostly because she didn't know it was me. As we walked together, she remembered. She needed to get involved. She was one of the girls who would be challenged in her years to come.

"I think you should be on flags Reevie." Miss Carol put her to waving the flags, which was new even for them. "Pastor is going to allow us to perform on a Sunday morning. You should do the flags." It was because of Reevie looks. She was not only beautiful but quite physically mature for a girl her age. Miss Carol didn't say it, but she thought Reevie would be a distraction to the men at the church. They didn't have proper attire yet and there was no hiding her.

Debut Sunday came. The dance team with flags was to enter as a processional with the choir. Pastor wanted pageantry the first Sunday. He wanted it to be like David's processional into Jerusalem with the returned of the ark.

Choir, dancers, flaggers. There was awe in the place as worship was thought to be engaged. Interrupted subconsciously—when Reevie, in her form fitting blue chiffon dress, began waving her flag. Hers said—HOLY IS THE LORD.

It wasn't her fault. She was just Reevie the way God made her. It was just that some of the men in the church, and some of the women, didn't see it that way, focusing on the pretty, shapely, young girl from next door, rather than the banner she was waving. And some of the flaggers, did think that waving the flags was actually causing some move in the Spirit beyond the desire of the Holy Ghost's own readiness to manifest.

Craig was visiting because his girlfriend was on the program. The church was small and to compensate all the dancers in the routine, the group of twelve moved up and down the aisle to accomplish the routine. There she was. She was gorgeous. She hadn't done this in a while. Years and perceptions had changed since she was a teenager. Her friend Ginger had convinced her go back, get connected in, follow her calling.

Things had changed. Dance ministry was now more accepted church wide. Almost every church had a dance ministry of some sorts. It had to be the discerning of Holy Spirit that had taught men and mothers to focus on the heart and message of the dancer. The other thought was that there was just so much sensuality in the world, and the church, that church folks had just become sensually numb.

Reevie was herself, her looks and nature. Unconsciously, one of the girl's dress was up to her thighs. The men had learned not to look at that. Some did mental and spiritual gymnastics in their head quoting scriptures and imagining that the lady of question was their daughter, mother or like the word said their sister. Other than that, they'd glance at their wives or suddenly get a scripture to look up. No one really knew totally what the single guys thought. Some thought, it came just short of a club experience at church.

Every move must count. She danced for her stepfather, enticing him. Her perfume heightened and released with every twist, twirl and twerk. The request for her first century lap dance was pre-set at the price of whatever she wanted up to half the kingdom. It was a ploy and it was going just as planned

She was giving her daughter pointers on how to seduce her husband and Salome's uncle. They consorted. "You can dance for him," whispered the evil queen veiling her voice, attempting to hide its demonic taunt. But the younger woman had already been possessed by knowing the king of Israel had been eyeing her.

"But you dance. Don't hold any things back. Make him want you. And when he asks you the cost of your pleasure. Tell him you want the head of the prophet, presented to you, on a platter."

Herodias, despised John the Baptist the fiery, Holy Ghost preacher. How dare he accuse her husband of sin? So what of the divorces—and lust over law—-marrying his sister in law. Herod Antipas feared John. He rather enjoyed his preaching. However, the enticement of his niece's dance and his own lewdness and pride, committed him to murder the prophet of God, the biological cousin of Jesus. It was King Herod's birthday.

Reevie was intentional this time, wearing one of her most form fitting outfit. If she was going to be blamed anyway, might as well go with it. Service had already started. The doors to the main sanctuary were shut. You weren't allowed in while ministers were praying. "Amen" followed by a louder congregational "amen" was released and the doors were open in the back to let the late comers in for service. She walked down the center aisle. She walked properly, she was descent. It was just the dress. Five inches above the knees and the "V" top blouse showed the way. The usher was no wise smarter leading her almost to the front row.

"She can sit here," whispered a voice from the second row, on the right. Mother Dixon was the wiser, discerning possible intentions, and of course general wisdom of sight. She scooted over and allowed the young woman, who hadn't been to church in thirteen years, to set down. "It's okay, honey," whispered the seventy-five-year-old church mother.

Reevie wasn't going to originally, but wriggled her dressed down, from the hem, with both hands, forcing it to reach two inches above her knees. It had traveled up her thighs. Only nine-year-old Stephen, across the aisle, noticed her dress, and thighs. He was still too young to know about impropriety or what older church women would call a Jezebel. Still he smiled. Reevie reminded him of his Aunt Joyce from Ohio and she was pretty.

Truth was, it wouldn't have affected Pastor Tye. Him and first lady Karen were closest ever—a model of marriage. But greater than that, pastor was sold out. He talked often about his earlier street evangelizing days, ministering to prostitutes, going into strip bars getting the girls saved. This Sunday he preached on the love of Jesus for all, but highlighted the tough love of the Holy Spirit, not only to save, accept, but to change.

It wasn't long before Reevie, began to get hot. A droplet of sweat formed around her right temple. Both ears were burning. She twisted more trying to pull her dress down. Mom Dixon knew it and handed her a shawl to cover her legs. Why did she do it? She knew better. She knew what was appropriate and not appropriate for church. Her mother had schooled her on when and where. Reevie stayed through all the message, and when the altar call came, she went up. Mother Dixon went with her.

Craig couldn't stop looking at her. The dancer with the short dress wasn't noticeable to him. "They all dress like that?" he subconsciously thought. The flags were twirling in patterns it seemed. One twirlers stopping another beginning all down the line. Suddenly, the course would change like a wind. Then for no apparent reason one flagger would run, drop their flag, and exchange for another, choosing flags like choosing weapons in battle for the right one to hit the designated target.

The band played the style—a worship, rock, Jewish mix.

KING OF KINGS LORDS OF LORDS, THE LION, THE LAMB, RIGHTEOUSNESS

The words of the clapping flags all graced the place reminding the worshippers. Hands were raised. People danced in their place, as much as the seat in front and back of them would allow.

Reevie sensed Craig was looking at her. She wore purple a royal color. Lydia, a prosperous business woman, in the book of Acts, by her merchandising of it. it was believed that Esther the queen wore it.

"I'm focused. Focus," Reevie she said. They're not looking at you but worshipping with you. But they were looking at her. "Not my fault," she tried settling. "I am who God made me. I submit my body unto God as a living sacrifice. Men need to be delivered. Lord I give it to you."

Mr. Charles was invited to this service on Sunday afternoon. Siting on the third row of the wooden pews. He saw Reevie too. He admired her beauty, but was enthralled by her worship. He thought of the church as the bride of Christ, adorned in God's glory, dancing in oneness with the Lord. He pulled out his handkerchief and wiped his eyes.

What Reevie, at that moment, didn't know, it wasn't her physical appearance that this time had fixed the gaze of the men and the others, it was the presence of God that was coming from her. Something different was happening. Worship had come home.

Pastor approved and the church invested in getting robes for the team.

11
Patty's Story

Red the New White

Diamond's dance was as flawless as it normally was. Not just a reflection of her hard work, practice, and discipline, but her dedicated spirit. She was in love with God. Her dance was her worship and her testimony. No one knew of her close call and how the enemy was trying to destroy her witness. Three things kept her. One, the Word of God she had inside, largely resulted of Sister Corinda's mentoring. Her father's love, and support, combined as number two. Number three her mother Miss Karen was relentless in prayer.

Patty's time on stage was about to come, just two after Diamond. She was important to me also. All the girls were. Patty was special. None of the rest knew, but I was cheering her on. I was watching her every step at practice. Not to criticize, but I knew every dancer's steps, before the curtain opened. I came to almost every practice and recital. I was familiar with all the routines. The truth, I wasn't at every practice. When invited I came. I'd been involved in dance ministry for a long time. And likewise with the recitals, they assuredly asked for my attendance.

The other girls could add lib if they forgot a step, but not Patty, knowing her steps and timing was critical to her performance. I would help her when she asked me to. Sometimes she did.

"Like this Patty" I move. She follow. Demi plie. Chase. Rond de jambe, Spin.

Sometimes she would listen. Sometimes she'd push me away. I had to stand off to stage right and let her dance alone making mistakes. I breathed heavy when sometimes she'd tripped over her own feet. Some of the other girls and teachers would hold in the chuckles. Not me, I loved her and would still be there if she fell. Not all the teachers or the students knew my thoughts. It was probably better that way. Ashamedly, everyone wasn't manifesting their Christianity.

Patty Rodriguez showed up two years ago at *New Hope's Dance Ministries* practice. She just showed up, not knowing to call first, to check the availability of joining the school, or the cost. Her friends or ex-friends called her Red. Her name given because of the blood she'd leave behind her. She had assaulted over twenty-three people. And in a fight, she almost killed a woman ten years her senior.

"Ain't nuttin Tosh wees going to eff those b's up tonight ain't nobody do us like that on our own block," Red was furious, but calm at the same time. She knew how to reserve her anger for the fight, let it build and then release it with her fist or knife.

"So what we going to do Red? Hit them in their place?"

"No, I would, but I don't know what they got. We going to be like Pearl Harbor and hit them when they not expecting."

"I get it Red. You thinking the mall. I know Rachael. She's been up at the Mall on Tenth Street with her girls."

"No, we are going to hit them Sunday morning."

"Sunday morning?"

"Yup... Little B goes to church with her Moms. We get them there."

"Are you sure Red? I mean that's church. We messing with the Lord."

"Look the way I see it, we'll be helping God out. Just one less B—down here messing with people. And when did you get so religious anyway. Your parents were Jehovah's anyway."

"I'm with you Red, but little kids be going to that church too. I saw that preacher there helping little kids. They be doing something good." Tosha Medley was called in her gang Tom Tom. Nobody was sure why. Red was the first to call her that, so it stuck. She followed whatever her leader said, but from time to time, like now, she'd speak up.

"Look we going after Rachael and her dudes. We're not trying to take out anybody else. But if anybody, including the Pastor, gets in the way. Got to do what you got to do."

"Before church or after?" asked Tosha.

"I'll let her get some Word in her before we do her. I mean I'm righteous."

Pastor Steve Jones struggled with preparing his message. He thought he had it on Thursday. Usually, he'd work on it Wednesday, in the evening, his study day. At least he would have the outline. He was awoken Sunday morning at three.

"I need you to pray," said the Spirit, forcing the pastor to open his eyes to check the clock.

Obedient, Pastor Steve prayed in the Spirit, first while lying in bed, then maneuvering his body until he was bedside on his knees. For some reason a fifteen year old church member Beatrice Connolly was on his mind.

Darkness painted his bedroom. The wall, the bed, and even the bumpy form protruding from under the covers, his wife was all one hue. Blinking his eyes didn't matter. After several times, he squeezed them shut tight and listened. "You're going to preach on the power of the Blood of Jesus," is what the preacher later reported he heard from the Spirit. "You are to take your message from the scripture where I cast the devil out the man with the legion. It will be an illustrative sermon so get ready."

Pastor Steve knew God's voice and new the scripture about the Gadara maniac. He knew about the man in the graveyard bound with chains. The demons in him were so many that the man broke the chains. He was running around, chains dangling, but still confined to the graveyard. He ran to Jesus. The head demon cried out to Jesus "Jesus of Nazareth why have you come to torment us before our time."

Pastor Steve didn't know what the Spirit meant when he said illustrative sermon. He was at this passage when Red and Tosha walked in and sat in the back row. The clan leader looked around until she spotted Lil B, and her mother, sitting third row, from the front. Beatrice—Lil B, didn't see Red.

"Jesus said to the demons in the man. 'What is your name?'

The demon replied, this time sounding like many voices, 'Legion for we are many.'

A Roman legion is about 6,000. There were thousands of demons and all in one man. This didn't faze the Master. Jesus told them to come out.

The demon came out, but not before asking Jesus permission to possess a horde of hogs feeding nearby. Jesus allowed this. The demons did so and the unwilling swine ran off a nearby cliff, into the water below and drowned.

It doesn't matter what's binding you up, one thing or many," bellowed Pastor Steve his voice was clear, and powerful at the same time. "The Lord has the power to set you free, if you come to him. So today, to those who are in this room, if Satan has been plaguing you with sin, fear, hate, or whatever, you can be free today, by the power of his blood, and by his name. I command the demons to leave you."

There was a scream. Tom Tom looked over and saw her friend and leader on her knees screaming.

"I want to be free."

Pastor Steve ran to the back row, deacons following. He stood over Red

"Daughter would you be free?"

Patty cried, "Yes!"

"Then call on Jesus to free you."

"Jesus save me", she shouted

"Come out of her," screamed Pastor Steve.

Patty jumped up, banging into the pews as if someone had snatched her up. She fell quickly on the floor with a bang. She looked dead—unconscious. Tosha was scared stiff. She was frozen, afraid to speak. She had seen a lot of horrendous and scary things. She had never seen or felt what she just experienced and what happened to Red. Patty, former gang leader of *The Eight Street Elite*, was free. She opened her eyes. There was smile on her face. The church was praying. One of the ushers who saw the gun in Red's back pocket called 911. The police were pulling up as Pastor Steve was leading Patty in the sinner's prayer.

The tear-stained cheek, surrendered, gang leader, was arrested still. Red was wanted for armed robbery of a convenience store the other night. They caught her on camera. They charged her for armed robbery. This one for just a pack of cigarettes. Her previous record and a couple of unresolved warrants caught up with her. The judge gave her ten years.

Pastor Steve visited her regularly. Good behavior, Pastor Steve's influence, and help from the Spirit, Patty was out in six months.

Like the man in the graveyard, Patty still carried the weight of her past. It was a miracle, but she was able to get free of the gang. Most of the girls had disbanded her any way after her arrest. Tosha Medley had actually started going to church. Not Pastor Steve's church, but her grand mom's church in Westville.

In every service Patty sat in, she kept hearing—guilty, guilty, guilty. The voice was so clear. Conversely, at the same time, she could hear another voice saying, "I love you." God's voice was softer though, and sometimes it sounded muffled in her mind. On Sunday evening, there was a special service. It had been almost a year from Red's encounter and plot at Restoration New Freedom Church, New Hope Dance Ministry came to minister along with a preacher. She had never been in a service with a dancer performing to Christian music. Marlene Gasby danced to Tasha Cobb's "Break Every Chain"

Patty didn't know if it was the song or the dancing, but freedom came to her. She watched as Marlene twirled, and glided, lifted her hands, and told a story of chains being broken. She could see it. It spoke to her. She saw herself dancing before the King of kings. She saw herself free. She couldn't get the image out of her head. When she went home that evening, she dreamt about it. But, it was herself dancing in her dreams. Jesus was in the audience and nothing else mattered.

So she showed up one afternoon to the dance studio seeking how to be a dancer. The only problem, Patty had never danced before. And there was a reason why. Patty, former gang leader—Red, was in a car accident at age six. Her father Jessy 'Maleek' Carter was driving. He was high on crack. Her mother Alisa Rodriguez was killed when her estranged boyfriend ran the red light and their Chevy Nova was hit by a truck. Patty's left leg was broken. Jessy went to jail for possession of drugs and paraphernalia. Patty now walks with a limp.

12

Loronda Dance

What Can We See?

Loronda walked to her spot and waited for the music to start. Mr. Charles breathed in and waited for the music. He recognized the song from the first bar. It was one of those anointed pieces that could carry the dancer.

The track must have been rerecorded or the sound technician hadn't had it fully queued. Loronda seemed to be standing there in position for a minute. Her legs seemed to shake as she held her pose. It was evident as soon as she walked on stage, but the musical delay gave him more time to think.

He couldn't help from noticing Loronda glasses. "Take the glasses off" Mr. Charles thought. "Unless you are legally blind you don't need them. They don't wear glasses on a Hollywood set." He physically shook his head trying to mentally clear his thoughts. "But we're not in Hollywood... let me focus on the message." Involuntarily, his eyes and mind went back to the glasses.

"These are some thick glasses girl," holding up her glasses to the light and then trying them on. "I think they use to call them coke bottles."

"You better not put them to the sun I think they burn your retinas." Cheryl responded to her brother Teak.

Lo Lo—what her sibs called her, was born Loronda Melissa Hardgrove. She was the middle girl in sort. She had an older sister, an older brother, and a younger brother.

"We're just messing with Lo Lo. You know we love you. Even if you can't see it."

Loronda smiled slightly this time. Mostly she ignored their comments concerning her eyes. She knew her brothers and sister loved her. They just like to pick. It's what they did. She had her time too. She would never say too much, but she did things. She put a fake worm in Cheryl's lunch. Or, the other day when she hid one of her big brothers' favorite sneakers and sat there and watched him look all over the house for it. She finally pulled it out, from under the pillow, she had been sitting on, and held it on her lap, smiling.

Teak was so mad "I'll get you Lo Lo" he said snatching the shoe form her lap.

Her eyes weren't that bad. The glassed did help and they weren't as thick as they use to be. God had healed her. The Hargrove's weren't totally sure why her sight hadn't completely restored, but they certainly weren't like before. Her father said that it was probably because Loronda had trusted so much in wearing the glasses. When she was ready to go all the way, she wouldn't need them at all.

At age twelve she woke one morning and complained about her sight. All of a sudden overnight it changed. "Momma everything is blurry."

"I'll called the eye doctor today and set up an appointment," consoled her mother. She went to school that day only to have the nurse call Mrs. Hardgrove during the day to come and pick her up. Her vision had become so blurry she could hardly see how to get to the class room.

Junior Macular Degeneration, Stargardt Disease was the optician first diagnosis. When the scan came back. He was not as positive. Dr. Murphy wasn't sure what it was. He said he never seen anything quite like it. Although there was evidence of cataracts, he didn't think it would have so suddenly caused the vision loss Lo Lo was experiencing. "We can operate and remove them but... I mean you can try a second opinion, but I have been doing this a long time."

The Hargrove's went to church often. Mom sang on the choir at the midsize Baptist church they attended. Never too much talk on healing. Only that God was able. And then some references to—His will be done. Her husband went less frequent. It wasn't that he didn't want to, but as a national salesman, he was sometimes away on the weekends. When he was home, he went faithfully taking his wife and three kids.

Ed was away when his daughter's eye sight failed and the doctors gave her the diagnosis. Mary Hardgrove didn't want to have her twelve year old operated on and especially not something dealing with her eyes. She started the car and headed home. She called her husband on the way. Both must have been listening to the same radio broadcast. Actually, Mary's radio was preset to 109.3 it was the local station WCTF.

She normally listened to the news on the way home, but she was hoping to hear from God. She believed the Christian radio station would get her in tune. Ed Hardgrove hit the scan button by accident trying to turn the volume down so he could talk to his wife on the cell phone. By the time he could hit the volume *There Is Healing In His Stripes*, by Jimmy Michaels, was playing stereo in his car and Mary's.

"The doctor says surgery may help but he's not sure. It's like something else is there."

There was a pause. "We'll get a second opinion," said Ed, regaining his composure, swallowing, and looking up in his rearview mirror assuring that he hadn't just run a red light.

Mary explained, reciting the doctor's report. "He said we can get one but it's going to be the same."

"Well look Mary, it's Monday. I'll be back in town on Wednesday. Its prayer night, we're going to prayer. We're going to get a second opinion."

Loronda could hear celebratory music mixed with "amens" and "hallelujahs" coming from the church auditorium they entered. She could still perceive the light and see cloudy silhouettes of objects. People were understood, because they were the objects that kept moving. The room seemed to be full with movement. It was unlike several years ago when her father came home from being a way a week.

"Loronda, Cheryl, Teak, your father said be dressed when he comes home we're going to church."

"Awl mom," Teak, the oldest moaned, shifted on the couch, still clicking the controller on the X box. "I have homework to do."

"Boy you're playing video games. I'll guess you'll have to do it after church."

"Dang! Last time it was boring."

"Loronda, I'll help you." Mom Hargrove redirected her conversation. "Just do what you can."

"Yeah, don't put miss match socks on," flipped her brother still clicking the controller.

Prayer meeting that night was boring by most standards. Wednesday service at Calvary Non-denominational was somewhat like a lot of churches. Half, sometimes two thirds, the congregation of Sunday. No band on Wednesday just a worship leader. Pastor Clift would teach about a half hour and sometimes a request for prayer. All in all, church was over in an hour maybe an hour and half.

"Anybody need prayer." Called the Pastor.

Ed Hargrove wasted no time. He nudged his wife. They both stood. Ed helped his daughter to her feet. "Yes, we do."

Pastor didn't know. "What do you need pray for Brother Ed?"

"My daughter Loronda has been diagnosed with congenital cataracts. She can't see. Only shadows. We're believing God for a miracle."

Pastor Clift swallowed. Caleb Burke, who was a twenty-year member, was half a sleep. He had a long day. Ed Hargrove's request woke him wide up.

"You said she can't see," repeated pastor.

"Yes!"

"When did this happen, Brother?"

"Last week, Pastor Clift, when I was away on business." He looked over at his wife. Mary nodded in agreement.

"So what did the doctors say?" The pastor was trying to get all the facts, but somewhat hesitating. He had never prayed for someone's eyesight before.

"They say they want to operate. But my wife and I..." He turned and looked at Mary again and waited for her nod. "We are believing for a miracle."

Pastor knew he was accountable to pray as the church's senior pastor. Which at the moment was his motivating force. "Can she walk? Can y'all come up?"

Loronda was a little offended thinking, "Is this how it's going to be? It's my eyes. I can walk."

She had already thought about riding to school in one of those special buses or walking down the road with a service dog and a cane. Occasionally, standing on the corner with a sign that read—*Can't Work, Give Money.* Now, she and her parents stood before their pastor. In some ways, it wasn't Pastor Cliff Simmons' fault. He never had experienced anything like this before. Although he was quite aware Jesus opened blind eyes.

"Father in the name of Jesus" He paused. "Church help me pray. Point your hands this way." He saw another minister do that one time, while visiting a Word of Faith church. He knew they believed in miracles. "I know Jesus is a healer and if you want to you can heal little Loronda."

"Little, I'm 12 years old," thought Loronda. Again becoming a little offended.

"Touch her Lord and if it's your will for her to go to the doctors give them the wisdom. Oh and give them wisdom to accept what they can't change. But let this work for your glory. In the name of your son Jesus. Amen."

"That's it," Loronda, her father, and mother all thought the same thing. So did Pastor Cliff. Everyone except Loronda peeked at her eyes hoping God had showed up. Loronda was expecting to feel a tingle. For a moment, she did, then nothing.

She thought, okay now what?

"The church and I will keep praying for you Brother Ed," consoled Pastor Cliff. It was his attempt to encourage. "Y'all keep your head up. God will help you."

Two years had passed since the first diagnosis. It was later determined that surgery may not help and could prove quite risky. The conclusion according to medical opinion was to live with it and hope for new treatment to come along.

The Hargrove's adjusted. Loronda kept going to school. It was her choice after she got over the initial self-pity and fear. Although her siblings looked out for her, life became a little slower and cautious. She had the dark spots from bumps and bruises to testify.

Mary became discouraged and slipped into accepting her daughter's disability. Ed Hargrove never gave up. He bought tapes and books from ministry that preached on healing. The CD player in the car almost always had a faith building CD in it. "One day my little girl is going to see again," he said envisioning the future of his daughter.

Tonight was different and unbeknownst to the Hargrove's Missionary Gary Johnson was the guest speaker. Gary was a tall, slender, man—dark complexion, mustache, and medium length hair, worn in a small afro. Usher Jeremy Nelson said, in appearance, he reminded him, of a lead singer, of a seventies group.

No one knew if Gary could sing but what was known is that he could preach and teach the bible. The Missionary would tell of speaking to tens of thousands on the plains, and in the bush, in places like Africa and India.

Miracles happened all the time. Blind eyes open. The deaf hear their children voices for the first time. The cripple walk. Sinners get saved. People would ask why are there more miracles happening in Africa than in the USA. The fiery preacher would always resound in a voice that would wake the dead. "It's not that God loves the Africans more, but perhaps they love him more."

He was referring to the approach that people in other countries would come to receive from God. They walk for miles and wait, standing for hours, before the meeting started. When they heard the call to come to the altar there was no hesitation.

"You have to come to God in faith. You have to believe that he loves you. You have to believe that Jesus gave life for you. You have to know that he has truly forgiven your sins. You have to believe that he bore your sicknesses and pain in his body with the stripes, slashes and open wounds. The beating he took, was his payment for your divine healing in full."

Loronda father wasn't the only one that continued to seek God. Pastor Cliff was so taken by what he called a pitiful performance in prayer. His lethargy led him to read, study, fast and pray. He believed, he had turned himself off to the power of God and had led his congregation wrongly.

It was during this time he stumbled over Gary Johnson ministry in an online magazine. The Google search phrase was "Holy Spirit Manifestations"

It was praise and worship. The band performed before Missionary Johnson ministered. Missy Eldridge was asked to praise dance. She was twenty-two years old, but looked sixteen. She danced to *There's Healing In This House* sang by Grace Larson Brumley.

Missionary Johnson later revealed, he wasn't moved by many praise dancers, but Missy's dance brought tears to his eyes. He said it set the tone. He said it wasn't because of her moves or even the music that touched him, but the scripture she read first.

A father had brought his son to Jesus after the disciples couldn't cast out the demon that trouble him for years. He asked Jesus to help his unbelief.

> *And one of the multitude answered and said, Master, I have brought unto thee my son, which hath a dumb spirit; And wheresoever he taketh him, he teareth him: and he foameth, and gnasheth with his teeth, and pineth away: and I spake to thy disciples that they should cast him out; and they could not. He answereth him, and saith, O faithless generation, how long shall I be with you? how long shall I suffer you? bring him unto me. And they brought him unto him: and when he saw him, straightway the spirit tare him; and he fell on the ground, and wallowed foaming. And he asked his father, How long is it ago since this came unto him? And he said, Of a child. And ofttimes it hath cast him into the fire, and into the waters, to destroy him: but if thou*

canst do anything, have compassion on us, and help us. Jesus said unto him, If thou canst believe, all things are possible to him that believeth. And straightway the father of the child cried out, and said with tears, Lord, I believe; help thou mine unbelief. When Jesus saw that the people came running together, he rebuked the foul spirit, saying unto him, Thou dumb and deaf spirit, I charge thee, come out of him, and enter no more into him. And the spirit cried, and rent him sore, and came out of him: and he was as one dead; insomuch that many said, He is dead. But Jesus took him by the hand, and lifted him up; and he arose.
—Mark 9:22-27

Gary preached on that scripture.

"The Word of God is the answer to unbelief. Like the sister that danced. Her dance moved in worship. In worship, we must connect with the Word of God, and the promises of God, and the Love of God. God is going to heal someone's eyes tonight. If that's you come on up"

Loronda and her father were the first one to the altar. Missionary Gary leaned forward. The worship music in the background became louder. Ed whispered something in his ear.

"Okay Lord," pausing a moment and smiling, "I'll do that." Before anyone knew it, the thin preacher had taken his bottle of water, dump it in his hand, and immediately splashed it into Loronda eyes. Water went all over Ed and hit the usher standing behind Loronda, as well as two people in the front row.

"Whu-aah!" Loronda gasped, immediately throwing her hands up to face to wipe away the water. "Oh my God!" she shouted, her voice now louder than the music, "Daddy, daddy, I can see."

Everything was just right in the windowless auditorium. The maroon stage curtains, and mahogany floor, the themed flats in the background were fitting to enhance a great performance. Tinted gels of different colors warmed on. The music began and the spot light illuminated the dancer's form. **Mr.** Charles back handed his eyes to wipe the tears. He neglected to use his handkerchief. Lo Lo had disappeared somewhere into the song. She was telling the story—Her story.

"That's it," thought Mr. Charles. "We're not the world. It's how he (referring to the Lord) sees us. It's ministry. And it's telling others wearing glasses or who have any other impairment that God can use them."

He smiled. Although, the next time he saw a dancer with glasses, he would have to struggle with it again.

DANCE RECITAL   TERRENCE G. CLARK

13
Candace Story

Thrown Away

A cold breeze blew. Minnie Bryant pulled her coat tighter around herself and then wedged herself deeper into her husband's arms. It was a good movie. Perfect for date night. "April was colder than normal this year," thought Minnie, but she said that last year. It was hard to remember sometimes. Cold felt cold and she preferred the warmer weather.

As they passed, she glanced into the window of the lit jewelry store, on the corner, catching the cubic zirconia display. "They leave those out in the evening." she thought. "They're not the real thing, but they're still not cheap." She kept looking out of the side of her eyes as they passed the alley. "What's that?" whispered Minnie, lifting her head and staring directly into the dark corridor. Not hearing her muffle, Richard loosed his wife slightly, thinking she was trying to reposition herself in his arms. But when she didn't, he asked, "You okay?"

"I thought I heard something in the alley."

"Probably a stray cat," responded Richard.

"No, it sounded like crying."

They had stopped, and backed up one pace. All the while, she looked deeper into the dark corridor trying to see what was there. There was a big trash container. Some old newspapers and debris laying on the ground. It was darker the further you looked back. Their shadows along with the illumination of the street lights pushed in at the opening. A fire escape, half way back, apparently connected the apartments over head to the ground. And, there was the back door entrance to Megantel's Jewelry store.

She heard it again... It sounded like a baby crying. "Ricky this is crazy. Let's go and look into the trash bin. That cat sounds awful like a baby crying."

Ricky was unsure. A chill came over him all of a sudden. He respected his wife and he knew he was supposed to protect her, but he didn't really want to go into the alley—baby crying or not. Courage rose in him, glancing quickly at his wife, sucking in some cold air and raising his left eye brow he went in. "Stay here and look out." He told his wife pushing off from her confidence in him to handle what may.

It seemed to be darker as he approached the bin and what seemed to be a baby crying. He slowly pushed his head over the top of the square greenish metal canister and looked in. Ricky Bryant didn't have to search with his eyes long. Disposed cans and bottles somehow were able to capture light from somewhere and illuminate certain contents inside the rusting canister. Wrapped in a blanket, but laying head down was a baby. "Call 911," he hollered back to his wife as the chill came back under his coat. He scanned the area again to see if anyone was there.

Minnie could still remember the lights, the sirens, the police, the paramedics and all the questions that were being asked them. "What did you see? Do know the child? Where were you coming from?"

They followed the medical team to the hospital. They were concerned about the child. "How could anyone?" she thought. "A baby. I mean there's child services," she spoke out loud to her husband.

"I know dear... but there's a lot of hurting, messed up people out there. Abortion after the fact you know," answered Richard as the two sit in the waiting area right outside of Emergency.

"They adopted me," said Candace. "I was the child in the dumpster. My biological mother threw me out like a piece of trash. And although my adopted parents loved me and raised me as their own, I had to deal with those thoughts in my life.

Some of you may look at me and say, 'wow she is so successful.' Yes, it is true. For those of you who don't know me, I am COO of iPEC, the number two communication company in the world. I don't always share this, but I gross 750k a year, not including a company car, stocks, revenue sharing, and other upper echelon perks. I also own interest in several internet companies and I have my own product line in an area I won't disclose at this time. But none of that is important. Yes, it is a blessing. For me, it is a testimony of what God can do in the life of somebody that the world or even family rejected.

And yes, I am a dancer. Well, I am a worshipper first. My dancing tells my story. This is why I do what I do. Firstly, it is to give praise and honor to my Heavenly Father. Secondly, it is to encourage people through dancing that they can rise up out of every situation and be what God has called them to be.

Tonight, when I got off the plane, after flying back in from Houston, I didn't know if I would make it on time.

Somebody rumored there was an accident. My plane was delayed because of a fire on the runway. Apparently, a smaller plane ahead of us crashed landed. Thank God there was only the pilot on board. Thank God he was alright. But that delayed us. You know, we all say this, and it's true, 'what the devil meant for evil God turned it for good.' If I was earlier, I may not have been able to have an answer for this young woman."

Now perplexed and pressed for time Candace Bryant speed walked through the airport to the valet desk to have her car brought to her. "That's right I parked it myself—Oh sugar! I don't know what I was thinking. I never park it myself. Anyway, I'll just give them my keys." She looked up and saw the line ahead of her. "Oh sugar!" again using her favorite exclamation. "I'll walk. It's not that far. I'll get to the recital soon." She headed toward the park garage.

"I can't believe they finally brought the recital to Jersey and I'm late. I'm out of town. Go figure. Lord what you trying to say." If anyone believed that God always had a purpose for everything it was Candace.

"Ah-men! Here's the elevator." Surprisingly, there was no waiting. She pressed the 'up' button, entered when the doors opened, pressed number seven, waited for the elevator jerk and sighed.

"What a day. I got to lay all this aside, like always. I got to dance for the Lord. And my feet hurt. But it will be alright. It always is."

If anybody knew how to switch gears and compartmentalize, the young executive did. Although times it was tough staying focused, she learned how to lay one thing down and pick the other up. Psychologically, multitasking was a great business skill to master, but that wasn't really how she did it. She simply trusted in the anointing. Some people used that word frivolously or casually, but not Candace. People always called her successful, but she would have rather them just called her anointed. They did, when she danced, but she yielded to God in all her life. "I really got to trust you God. Holy Spirit you always been there for me. It's all about Jesus any way. I got to believe somebody today needs to be blessed by the ministry you have called me too."

The warm breeze hit her face when the door opened, probably because the seventh floor was above the other buildings at the airport, and the air flow wasn't restricted. Exiting the sliding doors, the location where she parked downloaded into her memory and she turned right heading to section 'G'. Candace notice to the right, between a dark blue Hyundi and a late model opal Mercedes, a young women cuddling what appeared to be a baby wrapped in a blanket. It was. She kept walking.

"Miss, how you doing?" The young women spoke. Candace spoke back but kept walking. A little faster now.

"She's going to ask for some money," thought Candace.

"And it wasn't that I wouldn't have entertained that but I was trying to get here." Candace address the audience. The room was eerily quiet but filled with electricity. Everyone was waiting for her next word. "The woman called me again."

Hallica Miles, on the street she was called 'Que' because things always started when she showed up. She wasn't a party girl, but people just liked her. Que always had someone in her company. Still, it was a surprise to everyone when the sixteen-year-old got pregnant. Of course, no one knew. She carried small. Through the winter months, she always wore a coat. The hazel and cream complexion girl with ashy cheeks wasn't asking for money for cigarettes, drugs or alcohol. She really was looking for food. She just figured that putting money as a value would help to assure her baby's welfare.

"Thousand dollars for my baby."

Candace tried walk faster. A chill entered the back or her neck beginning a top her first vertebrate and spread quickly through her spine, shoulders, lower back, and forearms. Her next step was shaky. She heard a lot in her day, but this was the first. She stopped—about hundred feet past Que. "What did you say?"

"I am selling my baby. Do you want a baby? She beautiful. Look at her."

Candace looked around. Was there someone else around? Did anyone hear this other than her? Was there some dude in a hoody, around the corner, waiting to jump her if she stopped and engaged the girl?

Despite the nature of the engagement Candace felt a peace. Also, there was no one around to be seen. Which she thought odd since the lines were long at the desk in the airport. There wasn't even a porter getting cars.

"You are not serious," responded Candace. Her voice lifted to compensate the distance and a plane that was coming in to land.

"Yes, I am."

By now Candace had stopped and already started to slowly approach the young women. She was still looking around, confirming the premises. "Miss you can't be serious. What's your name?'

"Que."

"Que?"

"Yes. My real name is Hallica, but they call me Que."

Why are you out here selling a baby? Is it really yours? How old are you? You know this illegal?"

"Miss. I don't want any trouble. I just want my little girl to have a good home. You look like you can do that. I have her birth certificate. She's three months old. I can't take care of her and my family don't know."

"Look I can help. I am not going to buy your baby, but I can help, if you let me... If you are willing to try."

Everyone's eyes were still focused on Candace. She was the center of attraction. The dancing had stopped for a moment. Alicia Mantorano, twenty-six, from Bridgeport, Idaho was waiting on deck. She didn't mind. She was engulfed in the story too. However, before Candace next words, eyes shifted to a young lady entering the packed house, through the doors, mid-auditorium, left of the stage, the audience right. The girl in jeans, with a sky blue, nylon jacket, and a white t-shirt that you could partly see, was holding a baby.

"She listened. She's here with me tonight."

DANCE RECITAL   TERRENCE G. CLARK

14
Jose & Hayden

New Members

Jose was angry with his cousin. They practiced for months after deciding to participate in the recital. The two were close. He sensed something was off with her. When around him, she was quieter than normal. And Hayden always had something to say. They'd practice and she gathered her things and headed out. Whereas before, they would spend at least another hour talking before heading out. Talking, eating pizza, or a burger from *Mickey Dee's*. He was really blown off, after she kept hinting that perhaps he should find someone else to dance with.

Jose adjusted his back pack and looked down at his phone.

"I'm going to be late for practice be there in a half hour we need to talk." It was Jayden.

Pausing a moment on the sidewalk before turning into youth activity center lot, he texted back. *"Bring some chicken nuggets and an iced tea I'm starving."*

Cam, Reggie, Peter, Hassan were four of the five guys participating in the recital. David's dance was one of the models dance ministries used. His Psalms—149 and 150 were foundation scriptures. Still,
not too many males signed up. This year it was less. The four male,
teenaged group, comprised a single application.

NSTEP, wasn't really a playoff of the boy group *NSYNC*, it was a
reference to walking in accordance to the Word of God and the result-
ing blessings. The Philly group started in 2012, when Peter the oldest
was fifteen. They were being invited everywhere, following the local
circuit, but reaching out as far as Ohio. After the recital, an invitation
to Houston. The group turned down a request for South Africa a year
ago, not thinking they were ready. Someone from the country saw
their YouTube video and made contact.

It was hard for teenage boys. Most of the guys their age were
hanging on the streets or trying to connect with girls. Reggie's father
was the pastor and took the boys under his wings. He also was their
coach.

"You young men are awesome" He always made sure he referred
to them as young men. "There aren't many men of any age doing
dance...Well, singing either, or serving the Lord...At least not around
here...that I know of. But in order for y'all to do, what the Lord has for
you to do, you must stay before God. And, you must stay together. And,
leave girls alone, until God, not the devil sends the right one."

Everyone thought Reggie would be the one to most emulate his
father, but it was Cam. Cam Johnson was also the cutest—spiced skin
and chocolate brown eyes that blinked a lot when he first met some-

one, but stare wide open when he would talk about the Lord. Accordingly, he with all good intents tried to stay faithful. It was the girls that kept pressuring him.

Hassan, the youngest, usually had little to say but listened intently to what Cam and Reggie's father would say about God. He asked questions a lot, not because he didn't know the answer, but to get confirmation. If there was a challenge of someone debating the Word of God he was the one, who would wait his turn, and land the confirming punch.

"Y'all good." A crowd had gathered at Rothman Park. The group was practicing outside, getting ready for an upcoming event. They were clowning around at first. Reggie was running through a routine of dances. Hip hop, break dancing, and popular. Hassan was eating Chinese rice. Cam changed the radio noticing the crowd was really getting big. He had *Kurt Franklin's 123 Victory* already downloaded. It was the mix they were working on. He hit the play button and turned up the volume.

"Let's do this" Reggie started to move—the first steps in the routine, with a little freestyle hip hop added in. Peter bobbed his head and jumped up from the bench they were sitting on, jumping right in step with Reggie. Cam jumped in next falling right in time.

"Come on boy," Peter glanced at Hassan and back waved him to join.

The darker complexion curly haired friend washed down the rice in his mouth with a swig of Gatorade and jumped in last. Missing the first step but right on time after that. They performed the whole routine adding extra stuff throughout feeding on the Spirit and the atmosphere of the crowd

"Y'all good," the same voice repeated again. "What you doing with it?"

"Where praise dancers," Peter answered. A couple of 12-year-olds were dancing trying to entertain the dismissing crowd. The box was still playing a different gospel song, but Cam had turned the music down some.

"What's that?"

"They're a church group El." A girl next to him answered. "They dance in church for Jesus."

"What, y'all do that at church? Sounds kind of cool. Where's this church?

"Well were from different churches, but churches everywhere have dance teams."

"Yeah, but they're all sisters, aren't they?" Another voice spoke.

"True, in a lot of places. But we believed God called us to do what we do."

"But why y'all following Jesus and that religious stuff. That's limited. Y'all should be doing that sh-- on *American Got Talent* or something like that." Another voice spoke.

Cam spoke first. Yo brother. Dancing is from the Bible. In the Bible, God calls us to dance. God said in Psalms 149 and 150 to praise him in the dance. The devil perverted it and made it to something ungodly."

Cam was powering up. He was ready to go from scripture to scripture.

"Oh, here we go. I know about church." El's response at first seemed defensive. Contrarily, he wasn't disturbed at all. He was remembering. "My mom use to do the holy dance," he added.

"Amen, amen!" Cam was quick to acknowledge any response that sounded like an open door to talk about Jesus.

"Nah, she died. So much for that."

"I'm sorry brah,"consoled Cam, not moved by the damper.

"No, it's cool. It ain't you. But my point, y'all dancing for Jesus, when that's not gonna get you anywhere."

"Well first of all it ain't sh--. Its praise before the Lord and celebrating his goodness, so that people will know he's a healer." Hassan had opened his mouth and was about to keep going. Cam cut back in sensing the atmosphere heating up.

"That's Hassan," he quickly interjected. "What he's saying is that our dancing isn't necessarily for a show or entertainment. We do it because it glorifies God. We're glad people like it, but that's not our ultimate goal. We're sorry about your Mom." They all nodded in agreement. "I'm Cam. This is Reggie," said the assumed leader, pointing at each member of the team, "Peter and again Hassan."

"We just love the Lord. Can we pray for you?"

"Nah, I'm cool thanks anyway. But tell me where y'all be at and maybe I'll come check you out." El waved at someone across the street "Yo Kalleg wait up."

A blonde haired black girl standing next to him stayed. "Sorry about my brother. Our mother just died earlier this year. But, you can pray for me. I'm Lashea."

Lashea, El's sister was pretty. But the guys acted as if they didn't notice. "Are you saved?" Asked Cam.

"I'm not sure. We'd to go to church with mom. I asked Jesus to come into my heart. But still never experienced that peace I hear other talk about, including my mom."

Cam shared with the seventeen-year-old the Gospel using John 3:16 and Romans 10:9, 10. He shared with her how much God loved her. "I don't know why your mother didn't get healed, but I do know it was God's desire to heal her. And dancing like we do or the Holy Ghost dance won't heal or save you. It's faith in God Word that does that. Dancing is just a confident testimony that he has."

"Wow", exclaimed Lashea, she had never heard anything about Jesus quite shared like that.

"Do you want to make sure you're saved?" Hassan's voice was softer than when he spoke earlier.

"Yes," responded Lashea.

"Awesome," said Cam. "Let all join hands." He motioned to Hassan. "Why don't you lead? Lashea, our brother Hassan is going lead you in what is called the sinner's prayer, just believe by faith. Trust God in your heart that what he says is truth."

Before Hassan could pray Reggie spoke up. Smiling but seriousness on his face. "My sister do believe you are a sinner and need a savior."

"Yes," said Lashea, shaking her head in agreement at the same time.

"Do you believe that God gave and sent his only begotten Son Jesus Christ to die for the whole world including you as payment for sin," continued Reggie.

"Yes."

"Do believe what Jesus did settles your salvation with God for eternity and that there's nothing you could ever do to earn it?"

"Yes," Lashea's eyes were fixed on Reggie face

Reggie was done. Peter smiled. Cam nodded again at Hassan. "Go head brother."

It was Hassan, not Cam, who led Lashea into the kingdom of God.

Jose held the door for *NSTEP* when they entered *The King's Center*. They were distant friends connecting mostly at the annual recital. Sometimes included in a group list, when texting a holiday greeting or scripture. They sometimes hung out a little after the recital to catch up. Usually he, they, and Hayden would spend time at Rosetta's pizza and chill on the terrace, if weather permitted. But Hayden wasn't there this year as part of the duo.

"Hey bro where's your sister." Peter asked first.

Jose suspected that Peter always had a crush on his cousin but was scared to take it any further. Which, he thought, was cool. He loved it when everybody could just hang out as friends and not have any pressures of other relationships. However, *NSTEP* had a blonde-haired girl with them this year.

Although Cam never officially said that Lashea was his girlfriend. The way they acted when together sure set them that way. She was an addition to the group. Lashea came out and danced a duo part in their routine with Cam.

"Hayden couldn't make it this year. She's doing good though. It's complicated. You should call her though."

"Sure will. Got that Pete," said Reggie turning and looking right into Peter's eyes. They all laughed. Even Lashea who figured it out almost instantly.

"What?" questioned Peter, big eyed, before smiling from ear to ear.

Hayden was little over a half hour late, like she told her cousin. Adding ten minutes, stopping to pick up the nuggets, ice tea, and double cheese burger and coke for herself. She was still dressed as if coming to practice, back pack and all.

"Let's sit over here." She pointed to a table in the corner. The smaller gym where they practice for two hours every Thursday was empty. You could see people swimming in the pool, in the big gym, through the glass on one of the walls.

"Well I am going to come out and just say it." Hayden spoke first after distributing the contents of the food bag to the both of them. Jose had opened his nuggets and the smell of fried chicken quickly mixed with the normal gymnasium air. "I can't dance with you in this year's recital."

"Why not?"

"Because I'm pregnant."

Jose pressed his nugget deeper into the sweet and sour sauce cup before just letting it drown. In less than two seconds his demeanor has shifted from loving life to frustration. He snapped. "Hayden... No. What? How? Whoa...who? You don't know nobody."

Hayden announcement truly took him by surprised. Still, he was surprised he responded like he did. He always thought he'd be cooler than that. Many times, he had judged other people who responded to a friend or family member's situation judgmentally, particularly without first hearing them out.

"Jose cool down. I'm sorry. It just happened. I have been talking to people. You know."

"Yeah but, I didn't think nobody like that," rebutted Jose. "So, who?"

"Well you remember Malik from the basketball team in high school?" replied Hayden, jogging her straw several times in her soda before answering.

"Yeah, you guys use to talk for a little bit. On the phone and texting right?"

"Yeah but, he texted me last summer and we connected," voiced Hayden, with a little less passivity. "We went out a couple of times. One thing led to another and we... you know?"

"I'm still trying to figure just where I was when you were doing all this."

"I don't know," replied Hayden, her voice now softer sounding with remorse.

"But Cuz, we made a pact. Number one, we were going to honor God and wait until marriage. Number two, we were going to work this dance thing. Dance, teach... help kids. Ooooh Lord!"

"Jose I'm sorry. I didn't mean it to happen. I mean it's not over. I just got to deal with this. And I was hoping that you would be with me."

"I know," choked Jose. He had actually resolved his position two statements ago but was finding it hard to shifted the momentum. "Are you okay?"

"Yes"

"Is he still in your life?"

"Yes"

"Is he going to be there?"

"Yes"

"Is he saved?"

"Yes," answered Hayden, "that's one of the reason we connected. He works with the youth at his church. We actually went out first to a youth fun day."

"What kind of youth fun day was that?" said Jose sarcastically.

Hayden caught the punch, accepted it, and continued. "Us, locking up, happened several get-togethers later. We were at his parents' house alone. And...Jose, it just happened."

Jose finally breathed out air that was trapped in his lungs from when his cousin broke the news to him. "I know cuz. That's what usually happens, the enemy tries to come on strong to those of us representing. What can I do right now to help?"

"Just be there for me," answered Hayden. Her big brown eyes now lovingly looking right into Jose's, before dropping downwards. "And save that nugget before it gets soggy."

Jose laughed. He loved his cousin no matter what. He did have to find a new partner or go it alone.

15

Corinda's Dance

Words Can't Express

Dr. Janet Massie was exceptionally pleased with this year's recitals. Thirty-five teams registered. It wasn't that the dancing was better, but most of the dancers demonstrated a sincere heart for God. There were always going to be those who still didn't get it, coming for the contest. In some sensibility competition was still promoted by the recital. The reality, there were judges. Teams and individual were being graded in various aspect. Most points were not given for skill, but for presentation, with certificates including—sincerity, song selection, and outfits were several of the awards.

Corinda, and the doctor, thought about other models for the recital. Liturgical dance ministries could gather solely as a time to show praises to God. It would also serve as a time to encourage each other's gifts. After prayer, the consensus—the awards served as a regulator to give your best to the Lord.

The two matriarchs, and several others, began planning usually days after the end of the last one, allowing just a couple of days, to tie up loose ends, file receipts, balance the books, and send checks to the paid particulars of the event. The building was the biggest expenditure, followed by any equipment rental, extra security, catering for the green room, and the DJ. Time in between planning, was also unofficially allotted for rest, relaxation, and sipping ice tea around somebody's pool.

Additionally, The Dance Recital wasn't anybody's full time job. Corinda had her school teaching career, Dr. Massie was over the Psychology Department at a major hospital. The judges were selected from various non-participating entities—dance schools, fashion companies, and charities from across the countries. Airfare, hotel stay, food, and free advertising was what they received for their professional savvy. Everyone else volunteered their time. Most were there because they believed they were making a difference in the kingdom of God. They believed, the recital helped churches and Christians perfect their worship or was making a difference in the individual lives of the participants.

The recital's costs were offset by the registration fee for the groups participating and the sponsor supports from Christian organizations, business and ministry. Vendors' spots and tables were also available. The events would not just be jumping with dance, but hopeful merchandisers sporting everything from dance gear to nutritional supplements. Candace's company was a big supporter vendor and sponsor. Dr. Massie suggested it was getting a more commercialize every year, but resolved to the fact that patrons were still interested in coming to a Christian event. The auditorium held 2,500 and at 15 dollars a tickets the normal 90 percent of capacity also helped. So-called excess money went to the scholarships fund and the kick start fund for upcoming programs.

In previous years, the recital hosted at least one well known gospel artist. This also help to attract attendees. *Tamela Mann* was the requested artist this year, but her schedule wouldn't fit and the other choices also were already booked. Inevitably, this year's recital rested on its own laurels and the unction of the Spirit of God to persuade hearts to come. Several local and lesser known artists were still invited to perform. Dr. Massie and Corinda both believed it was God ordained, recognizing it gave several local ministers opportunity. Some as talented and anointed as their recorded counter parts, but just looking for the open door. And though, they received a small honorarium, their cost was a lot less than the more known artist.

"Vince hold down the table for me," Pastor Derrick Wynell pulled his Bose studio headphones off his head, and motioned to his partner. "I have to hit the can real quick."

"Uh okay," came back the response. "Everything in order? Anything I should know?"

"No...you're good, the next track is already queued. I'll be back in a minute."

Pastor Derrick had been there all day. His second job. He had turned tables and dropped music it seemed all his life and knew every chapter and verse of the profession. He never had formal music training, but the many hours listening to and queuing songs and tracks, he believed, he could conduct a symphony orchestra.

Vincent Cambry was his student. Twenty years younger, the twenty-five-year-old had a strong love for music, but still hadn't grasped the power of it. That's where his mentor came in, teaching him not just the power and placement of a song, but how music could change a mood, set a course, and even in the real world, score someone personal life.

I introduced Corinda and Dr. Massie to Derrick's ministry. They tended to listen to me. It wasn't just a personal preference, he had the credentials, the experience, and the equipment. King's Auditorium was audio ready, but Derrick's equipment was better. He knew how to make it work. Although, most of the music was prerecorded, it was as if he had written and recorded each song.

Not all liturgical dancers understood that there were basically three types of dance interpretation. One form you acted out the song. There was movement for every word. In this form, the dancers sometimes waited for the words in a song. The challenge, if there wasn't an immediate connecting phrase, the routine became too fractured. In the second form, the dancer just worshipped with the music. The movement didn't always connect with the words of the song, but the song was used to tell a story that connected with the song. The third was more artsy. It was beautiful and skillful, but sometimes too much concentration on routine negated the heart of the message.

Skill versus story was sometimes the dancer's dilemma. I understood the desire to give God all and to let him be Lord in all things, including dance performance, not all did. Although, it had its place, some still considered it showy and vain.

It wasn't another form, but dance with no heart or story was sometimes presented. It was one thing to see a newbie who was stage-shy, but a seasoned dancer without a story was one just literally going through the motions. It was another things that got to Mr. Charles. He hadn't been in the liturgical dance arena nearly as long as me, but he shared my passion.

I knew Praise Dance should tell the story of the dancer's engagement with the song, not a verbatim exercise to the words, or just a gymnastic routine. The balance of the praise dancer sometimes was all three. The greatest dance was when anointing and testimony harmonized together. Even the men, could dance like David and Miriam when celebrating God's triumph and presence. Ginger was exceptional in this. Miss Renny—what her students sometimes called Corinda, taught it to perspective dancers.

Vince started to sweat. He couldn't find Corinda's music. There wasn't any. Corinda walked to the center of the stage, looked up as towards heaven, smiled, and bowed her head. Vince started to panic. He looked towards the door where Derrick had gone through for the bathroom. He smiled when he saw his red and white small checkered shirt, but when the full body protruded, it wasn't Derrick.

Corrie, what her father use to call her, smiled relaxed a bit. She looked to the audience and suddenly begins to move. Vince looked towards the door for Derrick again and spotted him. He blew air through his gathered lips and almost whistled.

"I apologize I took longer than I thought," explained the older DJ to the younger, after approaching the sound platform and pulling his chair back. "All day you know..."

Vince interrupted, "I couldn't find Miss Corinda's music and she's on stage."

"And that would be because we don't have..." Derrick slowed his words, trying to remember if he forgot something. "Oh, it's here on the thumb drive."

"But she started. What do we do?" questioned Vince.

"I don't know. She started...try to get her attention."

The sound booth was set on a raised platform, half way back of the main auditorium. They both looked towards Corinda hoping to catch her looking back with some motion or gesture. But she was into her dance moving as if music was playing. Finally, as if it had been rehearsed, she returned to her starting place at center stage, now motioning towards the sound men to start the music. The audience was entranced. She could have kept going in the silence. Everyone thought it was part of her routine. It wasn't mime either. No choppy repeating movement—just a story. And, the people were getting it.

Corrie told of the story of the night she had been sickened by drugs and alcohols. She told of the life she was living. It was the night she turned on the TV and got saved listening to a Televangelist. She told her testimony in a dance. It was a song with no music. Miss Renny began acting out that night she came home. Afterwards, the music played and the worship began.

"Dancers what would you do if your track doesn't play and you don't have a backup? What do you do if your track stops in the middle of your song?"

"Panic," said one of dancers at the workshop Corinda taught.

"You stop and wait until they get it fixed," said another.

"Well that's a thought," the teacher answered. "How about just keep dancing and flowing in the Spirit. That's why when you dance for the Lord you need to be able to tell your story. To tell your story you need to know your story... And yes it is wise to always bring back up music"

I had seen the dance before. The first time in 1983. It was at A little church in Collegetown New Jersey. It was seventh on the program for the church's variety drama ministry program. Although this time with music. The song, *Words Can't Express*—by a group named *Nicholas*.

Interpretive Dancing was rarely performed in that day in churches. If it had not begun under the auspices of theatrical ministry, it may not have been allowed at all. Only a few other ministries around the world had liturgical teams at that time. Other than that, Christian dancing was only engaged when children trained in the performing arts of ballet, tap, cheerleading, and gymnastics.

Social dancing was either accepted or taboo depending on the denomination. Disapproving rules were strictly followed or done with don't ask, don't tell. It was warned, in some churches, that moving the body in rhythm, to any secular music would land a person in hell, or the devil clutches. The only other dancing in churches was the Pentecostal experience, when someone got what was known as the Holy Spirit quickening, these worshippers would dance—shake, skip, twirl, leap, all under the power of the Spirit.

It sometimes depended on the reigning ethnicity of the church that set the dance mode. Most of the black churches moved in sync with the music. Every clap and foot tap followed the upbeat or downbeat of the song. And if you were sitting in a certain section that whole section moved in harmony. Although it wasn't true, it often seemed that everyone could carry a note. Songs had leads, and verses echoed from the choir and congregation. It was beautiful.

Anglo churches often were more reserved, even in musical churches. Parishioners would clap with hands pressed together, singing songs from the hymnals through falsetto voice with trace of baritones, in a sea of sopranos. It was beautiful. The Hispanic churches spurned the double step pattern with feet and body ready to go into a full swing at any moment. It was beautiful.

The mixed churches I loved, like Dr. Stanley's. His church was eclectic with afro American, Nigerians, South Africans, European Americans, English from England, Italian from Italy, Spanish Americans, Spaniards, Haitians, Jamaicans, Sri Lankans, Puerto Ricans, Mexicans, Chinese and more. The music was mixed and so was their dance of praise. It was beautiful. Worship, in non-denominational churches with full bands, the congregants loved to dance—with jumping, skipping and bouncing. It was beautiful.

Mr. Charles would often remark that no one could dance like a white man. He was being stereotypical, but in a nice way. Barring the guys from the entertainment world, he said, they mostly have no rhythm. So, when the Spirit of God prompts them to dance, they don't care how they look. It was all out for the Lord. It was like they're drunk. It was beautiful.

For me, the key to all dancing, regardless of the tempo of the song, was the worship. I love all the dancers, but I think only Corrie (and Ginger), at this time, could do a silent dance, live on stage.

16

Epilogue

Beyond the Dance

"I did alright I guess," muttered Tiara, to her longtime friend Ravine.

"You did good girl."

It had been a long day. The program was down to only five more girls, a team performance, and then the acknowledgements, awards and other closing ceremonials.

Tiara and Ravine stood outside the side door of the auditorium. Someone had propped a metal chair in the arch to keep the door from locking backstage attendants out. Tiara sipped on the cherry coke she had been sipping before her performance. Ravine, pretending to look at her cell phone, commented under her breath negatively about one of the dancers outside smoking a cigarette.

"I mean it didn't feel like it used too," continued Tiara.

"Yeah, you been saying that for a while." Ravine posted back, still agitated that someone would dare smoke right at the recital. Her disgust wasn't so much because of a spiritual disgrace, but that the girl was violating her body. Despite the little unhealthy things she did, here and there, the fellow dancer considered the dancer's responsibility to protect their temple. "We better go back in and get ready. The team will be up in a little bit."

"Have you seen Donjae?" Asked Tiara, sheepishly trying to hide her fondness for the new girl with concern. "She said she'd be here."

"I thought I seen her out in the audience. I don't know, "answered Ravine.

Tiara lowered her voice. "That's a shame about what happened."

"You mean about Miss Candace."

"No, that turned out good, awesome actually," sighed Tiara, smiling.

"Yeah I know. Miss Candace has always been a good role model and good example of a Christian woman." Responded Ravine candidly before blurting. "So what you talking about then."

"You know with Donjae."

"Tee, I know you have taking a liking to her and so have I, but Donjae just needs our Christian friendship right now," counseled Ravine. She wasn't always spiritually conscious, but this was one of the times.

"I feel somewhat the blame, continued Tiara. If I hadn't of wanted to go to that place that night. She probably wouldn't have wanted to go."

"But nobody told her go back and back by herself on top of that," reminded Ravine, fanning her nose with her hands as if the cigarette smoke was bothering her. "Yeah, uh, who knew the place was going to get raided? Under age kids in there doing weird stuff. And, Donjae with that *girl*...caught on the news...ever find out who that *extra* was?"

"Wait Ravine, she said everything was cool. They were just dancing together."

"Same girl, I think she was dancing with the night we all went. But they were up on each other pretty tight. Personally, I think she likes you," postulated Ravine.

"Don't start that again. She just needs a friend."

Turning her one-year-old on her lap, and pointing towards the stage, Hallica Que Resposita was hoping her little one could understand what was going on, or least catch the image. She herself had never seen anything like this. It was beautiful. The music and dance flowing together spoke to her. There was something about the atmosphere. It wasn't church, but if it was as the emcee cited, "We're having church up in here." She wanted to be a part of this church thing.

Hallica was experiencing the love of God, again and again, through every dancer. In the three to seven minute choreographed presentations, somehow each dancer's life story was coming through. And that's what I always saw. I love music. I keep it all around me. But the real music was in each dancer's story told again of how they had been helped, delivered, saved by the power of God. They honored me throughout the day. They asked me to speak several times during and again at the end of the event. Right before Mr. Charles closed out the dance recital with prayer. I loved to hear Mr. Charles pray. He always knew how to talk to God and would take the time to declare a blessing on everyone the Spirit brought to mind.

I didn't really have a favorite. I loved them all. Okay, Patty's dance was intense. She had come out of so much and although skill-wise she was far from the top, her story was so powerful. Dori's dance was right there as well. Her golden age still expressing the youthfulness of her love in the Spirit. Okay, Corinda, Rita and her step-daughter Crystal, Ginger, Reevie, Loronda, Candace, Alicia, Tiara, Ravine, Tanisha Green, sisters—Janivera and Jantasha, Tamera, Carrie, Nessie Smith Colby from Dallas, Zeesia Lothens, Shante, Evelyn, Jose, Phyllis, Regina, NSTEP, and all the ensembles, I loved.

I did miss Donjae's dance. She should have been there, on stage, instead of out in the audience. Really that's how those things start. The condemnation of past sins. The hurt of rejection and not knowing how to deal with prevailing haunting thoughts.

That's where sin starts. In the head, it's a song that won't seem to go away and is eventually danced out. But the dance before the Lord, always overrode everything. Especially when it was done first in that secret place, allowing the Spirit to fill up, wash out, and conquer all the missed steps of sin. Truthfully, that's what I always look for in a dancer. Dancing was fun and I have danced playfully with some of the greatest. I knew when it was a dance of tears or laugher that is fine-tuned, and on point, by the Word of God. Still, Deacon White was angry with me. He hadn't been to church in three years.

"Things have changed," confessed the deacon to Mr. Charles, while they waited together in the barber shop.

"How is church?" Mr. Charles had asked. He hadn't seen the deacon in twenty years it seemed.

Wrestling with himself Mr. Charles didn't know whether or not he wanted to engage the conversation. Without Deacon White even saying anything, he knew what he was talking about. The liturgy he was accustomed to had changed over the years. Praise and worship services, had a different flow. The eighty-five-year-old deacon continued any way, "We had devotional services. The deacons prayed. We sang the hymns. The choir sang three songs. The preacher preached and we had church. Now not only did they bring that be-bop into the music, they got the girls shaking their behinds and moving their bodies and calling it holy. Rev...." Deacon White looked at Mr. Charles, calling him reverend. He was, but most just called him Mr. Charles. "Rev...I don't think the Lord is pleased. They allowed all that stuff in church. We didn't have none of that. Then that new pastor came in."

Mr. Charles smiled from ear to ear, still wondering to engage the deacon. He was thirty years younger than Deacon Harold White but he remembered those days too. He recalled, they called the service before the message devotional. And though there was some solemnity in it, it was still far from biblical worship. And even if, it was to the utmost of reverence, he thought about the Bible's invitation to praise God with the whole heart. Everything he had read called for all the congregation to dance and rejoice. Psalms 149 came to his mind.

> *Praise ye the LORD. Sing unto the LORD a new song, and his praise in the congregation of saints. ² Let Israel rejoice in him that made him: let the children of Zion be joyful in their King. ³ Let them praise his name in the dance: let them sing praises unto him with the timbrel and harp. ⁴ For the LORD taketh pleasure in his people: he will beautify the meek with salvation. ⁵ Let the saints be joyful in glory: let them sing aloud upon their beds. ⁶ Let the*

high praises of God be in their mouth, and a two-edged sword in their hand; ⁷ To execute vengeance upon the heathen, and punishments upon the people; ⁸ To bind their kings with chains, and their nobles with fetters of iron; ⁹ To execute upon them the judgment written: this honour have all his saints. Praise ye the LORD.
—Psalm 149

Mr. Charles did agree, there needed to be a balance. Praise and worship had come along ways. People had become freer, awaking to the liberty of children of God. Religion of the old days bound people up, he thought. He believed, people suppressed things, back then, both good and bad. Sin was kept in the imagination realm and translated into lust. If it wasn't sex, it was perversion of other sorts, sometimes cultic practices.

Jimmy finished cutting the hair of the person in his chair, pulled off the bib draped around him, and slapped away the loose hair in the seat with it.

"Pastor, it's you." Pointing at Mr. Charles and then gesturing to the now empty barber chair. Jimmy liked calling Mr. Charles, Pastor. Mr. Charles smiled, got up, and took the seat, hoping the shift would shift the conversation with Deacon White. Nevertheless, it didn't.

"So, what you think about all this Rev?" asked the deacon.

"A little closer on the sides," was the response, but directed to Jimmy, who had started cutting, giving his regular customer—"the usual". Jimmy was waiting for the response as well. He had been to Mr. Charles' church and knew that high spirited worship, including praise dancing, was a part of the services. He smiled.

"I got you," assured Jimmy, still smiling.

"No one danced like Mother Paul."

It must have been a Holy Ghost word. Deacon White had cross-folded his arms tight over his chest, while waiting for Mr. Charles answer. His worn baseball cap was dangling in his hand. His partially bald head revealed. Trevor Wilkins, in the barber chair next to Mr. Charles' chair, broke from boredom to wonder why the old man needed a haircut. The atmosphere had changed. *Old Spice* and *Barbasol* mixed in the draft, as the door opened, and a customer came in. Deacon White pulled his arms tighter together and smiled real big.

"You know you're right. The woman could dance and boy did she have a testimony," added the deacon.

Mr. Charles continued, "See when you know what the Lord has done for you or what he has promised, the questioned should not be, should I dance, but why aren't I dancing? I was dancing the other week at church." The deacon refocused his eyes on the preacher.

"I don't know if you knew it or not deac, but I was diagnosed with Parkinson Disease ten years ago and the Lord healed me. Last Sunday, I was in worship service and I began to think about the cross of Jesus, and what he did for me. How he saved me, and healed me, and I began to leap and dance."

"See that's what I'm talking about, when it hits you, it hits you. I remember those days. I guess I'm just use to the old way. But I'm not going to fight God."

"Amen, but deac, I also found out, I don't have to wait for it to hit me. I can just dance and rejoice because it's true. My dance is my praise and my testimony."

"So where's you pastoring at Rev.? I'd like to come in visit."

Mr. Charles shared where he fellowshipped, but he didn't believe the deacon would really come. Deacon Whites barber was ready for him and the move changed conversation partners. All the same, Mr. Charles couldn't stop thinking about the conversation. He agreed with what the Apostle Paul wrote in Galatians 5:13—

> *For, brethren, ye have been called unto liberty; only use not liberty for an occasion to the flesh, but by love serve one another.*

He remembered the days, of some of the so-called Holy Ghost dancing. In some places, it was rigid and cold. With women, church sisters would encircle another sister's outburst of dance. The others sometimes feeding the action chanting—rebuke or encouragement— to *hold on* or to *let go*.

In some circles, the cry was to "spit it out" and they did. It was dancing mixed with exorcism. The dance of the Lord was always different when allowed. When the hallelujahs flowed from a joyful face instead of one with the appearance of pain, it was glorious.

It was the birthing of the dances of the eighties, thought Mr. Charles that brought back the stories of triumph. It was like the dancers—men, going before the battle, and the women dancing at the victory. It was Psalms 68:24-28, 150:4, Luke 15:25—

THEY HAVE SEEN THY GOINGS, O GOD; EVEN THE GOINGS OF MY GOD, MY KING, IN THE SANCTUARY. THE SINGERS WENT BEFORE, THE PLAYERS ON INSTRUMENTS FOLLOWED AFTER; AMONG THEM WERE THE DAMSELS PLAYING WITH TIMBRELS. BLESS YE GOD IN THE CONGREGATIONS, EVEN THE LORD, FROM THE FOUNTAIN OF ISRAEL. THERE IS LITTLE BENJAMIN WITH THEIR RULER, THE PRINCES OF JUDAH AND THEIR COUNCIL, THE PRINCES OF ZEBULUN, AND THE PRINCES OF NAPHTALI.

THY GOD HATH COMMANDED THY STRENGTH: STRENGTHEN, O GOD,
THAT WHICH THOU HAST WROUGHT FOR US.

—PSALMS 68:25-28

PRAISE HIM WITH THE TIMBREL AND DANCE: PRAISE HIM WITH
STRINGED INSTRUMENTS AND ORGANS

—*PSALM 150:4*

NOW HIS ELDER SON WAS IN THE FIELD: AND AS HE CAME AND DREW
NIGH TO THE HOUSE, HE HEARD MUSICK AND DANCING

—*LUKE 15:25*

Mr. Charles loved Jesus' story in Luke 15. He would tell it his way.

Benjamin had been talking to a few of his friends who had journeyed from town for various reasons. Some with the military, others on business—traveling with merchants. They told of the wonders of the world beyond the little village where he lived. His father's farm was thriving. One of the wealthiest around.

According to custom, on his thirtieth birthday, twenty-nine-year-old Benjamin, knew he could ask his father for his inheritance. The day came and he approached his dad. "I have these things I want to do, father, explained Benjamin that I can't do here. I love you, but my destiny lies out there. I believe I can make it."

Ben's father, Asa was reluctant, but yielded to his youngest son, providing him with his portion of the inheritance, laid aside for him and his oldest brother, since they were born. It was his, although Asa peers questioned him letting his youngest go, when helping to run the farmer, was the better succession.

"I got Daniel, my oldest. Danny will always be with me. I know."

Ben followed his passions, but with little planning and wisdom. He went from town to town, sustaining an entourage everywhere he went. Succumbing to frivolous living, wild women, mind dulling alcohol, he lost everything. His business affairs collapsed. His ventures failed. He became homeless. To survive, he took a job herding swine. Which was a detestable occupation for his religion—a Jew. Famished from not having enough to eat, he was about to chow on hog food. At that moment, the thought came. "I bet my father will hire me as a servant on his farm. I blew it, I know, but I'm hungry. Now is no time for pride."

He bundled his pitiful belongings and headed home.

Asa heard the stories of both—his youngest son's failures and thoughts to return. He met him at the gate. Before Benjamin could complete his remorse and apology, his father pulled in his arms, hugged him, kissed his neck, and loved him. "Bring me a clean robe. Kill the fat calf, we have been saving for this day. Son," he said to Benjamin, "here's my ring of authority."

Daniel was in the field, when he heard the sound of music. He questioned a servant. "What's going on at the main house?"

"Haven't you heard," replied the servant, "your brother Ben is returned. Your father has restored him and thrown him a party. They're partying now with food, music, and dancing."

Daniel was angry and wouldn't go in the house. Asa came out to inquire. "Why are you out here, son? Come join the party. Let's eat, be happy, and celebrate in dancing."

"Father, I never left you," responded Daniel. "I stayed and helped you run the farm. You never gave me a dinner, to invite my friends, and celebrate with music and dancing."

"Daniel, nonsense, look around you. I love you just as much. In fact, everything that is mine is yours. But look, your brother came home. He was as if he were dead and now he is alive. This is why we celebrate today. This is why we dance."

Mildred Turner dances all the time. Jimmy Jr., her grandson, shared his dream. He saw Big Momma, in heaven dancing with Jesus. According to him, his grandmother looked like his mother. She was young looking, with shoulder length hair, which bounced and swayed as she danced. She died in 2009 when Jimmy was eight. Diabetes had taken away her legs. First the left, then the right. She never lost hope and would tell her grandson, "One day in heaven me and Jesus are going to dance."

"You don't got no legs," acknowledged little Jimmy, not trying to be disrespectful to his grandmother, he just didn't see what she saw. Jimmy also saw his grandmother dancing with a young girl about twelve. Jimmy didn't know, but it was his grandmother sister, Emma, who went to heaven at twelve.

Three days had passed since they all met in the children hospital in Delaware. Cameron and his wife resolved, if God were to do it, he would have to do it without the tubes. Shyra, was only two when she went to heaven. She was born with a whole in her heart. The first operation was successful. The second six months later didn't go as well. It complicated, with a stroke. The doctor said she was brain dead.

Tommy, her father's father, the preacher, prayed on the way home from Washington DC to NJ to pick up his wife and daughters. He along with the rest of the family and several prayer ministries were believing God for a miracle.

"This little piggy went to the market and this little piggy stayed home."

"Why are you giving this to me now?" asked Grandfather Tommy, talking to God, as he stepped his left foot out of the car. He had paused a moment, after parking, in the medical facility's parking lot, wondering why God had brought the nursery rhyme to his heart. Saying nothing to anyone, he joined his wife and daughters at the reception desk, and headed to the elevator. Cameron open the door of the room. The family had been living at the Delaware children's hospital for the past week.

"There are tubes everywhere and she motionless," he said, preparing his mother, father and siblings for what they were about to see. Sanitized and donning hospital gowns, they entered the children's intensive care unit, looking past the huge machines and small cribs, focused to where Shyra laid. Cameron did a good job of preparing, but the gloom of the whole room was still strong. Rev. Tommy stayed focused and unmoved. They all gathered around her little bed. Tubes coming from somewhere, disappeared into Shyra's little chest. Nina, Cameron wife, pulled back the tiny blanket from her baby's feet. Tommy heard the song again.

"Okay, Lord I'll do it," spoke Tommy. No one knew what he was talking about.

Starting with the big toe on his granddaughter's left foot. "This little piggy went to the market and this little piggy stayed home...."

That's as far as he got.

"Look," someone shouted.

Shyra's eyes opened, big. She began to look around.

"Call the doctor," shouted the nurse. We need a second opinion."

Shyra had heard her grandfather song. As he was obedient. God showed up as un-kosher as could be through a song about a pig.

The doctors pulled the tubes and called the family in the room. She still had life in her. Her were eyes closed as if sleeping, as if nothing was wrong, ready to awake for bottle or play. Cameron asked his father to do something, Grandfather Tommy avowed he would never do again and would never have to. He held his granddaughter and prayed with her as she went to heaven. No one knew, not even her grandfather, until later, why the miracle three days before, didn't manifest fully.

What Tommy saw, was Shyra (now about eight), her parents, and brother walking into a well-known fast-food restaurant. The one with the children's playground. The children were laughing, playing. Shyra pointed their way and said, "I want to go play." At her father's release, she let go his hand, and joined the other children. Today her little sister dresses up like a ballerina and dances to show tunes. Unaware that her older sister is in heaven, dancing the same.

I hung around a little bit after the recital. Derrick and Vince were of the last to go. After waiting for the auditorium to empty somewhat so they could pull up taped down cables. They loaded the U-Haul with speakers, mike and mixer cases, strapping the dolly to inside of the truck last. Vince was eating a sweet potato pie that a vendor had given him. He was explaining to Wendy, the twenty-four-year-old baker, how important the sound was. She had two pies left and mentioned he would like to try the pie.

I was glad, Corinda's husband Barry made it. He had to work at the last minute. At least that's what he told her. He didn't really want to come. He still felt jilted with her time away from him spent working on the recital. I had talk to him at Corinda request. Barry was a good man. I talked to his wife also. Corinda did need to spend more time with him. He walked in right when Zeesia Lothens took stage to dance. He recognized the girl from the school. Zeesia mother had heard about Corinda and her classes and signed Zee up. "Wow, Hallelujah, that girl can dance," exclaimed Barry. "She reminds of me Corinda."

Dancers had already signed up for next year's events. Dr. Massie and the team had locked in the Mt Laurel venue again, still believing New Jersey was the location to be. I thought it was. I was always good with locations, even when others disagreed. Another year here and then somewhere else. No matter where it was, at least for this season of Christianity, dance was an effective journey into worship. It also promoted team spirit, something missing in the church for so long.

Fourteen-year-old Kallie was excited to get to church on Sunday. She learned so much. The Spirit had rested on her at the recital. She didn't even care about her performance. She was just excited that she had the opportunity to grow and be filled. Although, it wasn't her Sunday to dance, but one of the other girls—Crystal. She was excited for her.

It was starting to get dark. The security lights at the center were already on but weren't noticed earlier. They began to glow and then become bright as dusk set in. I set on the bench outside again for a few minutes. The honeysuckle was still filling the air—as if for me.

I heard a sound and pulled myself to the edge of the bench. An apparition, maybe to some, but not to me. One dance more. Little Ezzie, Hallica's child had caught the glimpse. Her mother had almost given her a way. She spent the first months of her life on the street, not in her own bed, not in her own room—under blankets with her name on them. Almost miraculously, there she was dancing to a song that had not yet been written. I knew it. Her story had just begun. The music was queued. I clapped and smiled, like I had done for everyone's performance. I clapped again and cheered her on.

To Be Continued...

There's a recital being planned in paradise right now. Practice is going on right now as we visit. They are banners, flags, and everyone gets their turn. I'll be there to hear their story and cheer them on. Right now, you are preparing to go on stage at your church, school, concert, or recital or life. I'm ready to hear your story, testimony, praise, victory, warship, and worship in the dance. I'll be there to cheer you on.

17
My Story and Dance

Name

If you are a liturgical dancer, write your own chapter in dance ministry in this section by reflecting on the statements below. Add insights of your own. Tell your story.

I believe God called me into dance ministry because...

I want to dance for the Lord because...

The scripture I stand upon for dancing and ministering is...

The scripture I stand on for my life is...

My favorite song to dance to is...

I got saved (when & where)...

God delivered me from...

The current challenges in my life I am believing God to overcome are...

The area of my most spiritual growth since I began praise dancing is...

Person in the bible along with Jesus who inspire me the most...

Person in the current day who inspires me the most...

My most memorable dance experience was...(why?)

_____

_____

_____

_____

_____

_____

_____

_____

_____

_____

_____

_____

_____

_____

_____

_____

_____

_____

_____

_____

_____

_____

_____

_____

_____

_____

_____

_____

ABOUT THE AUTHOR

Rev. Terrence G. Clark is a preacher, teacher, author, playwright, cartoonist, and vocalist. In the early eighties, he was writing and directing a traveling church performance ministry. While preparing for a particular performance, by Holy Spirit direction, he introduced what is now known as liturgical dance to the regular program. The ministry was highly effective and became a regular part of the set.

One of the cast, a former secular performer in the arts, was to tell her testimony, without words, in a dance. The person, who ministered the dance, went on to teach this ministry throughout.

Terrence believes that it was through this ministry—the dance—God's dance was resurrected back into its rightful place. Terrence believes that although expressing the gospel through dance is holy, sometimes it is wrongly represented or engaged. Transforming, beyond the stage presentation, the greatest performance of the liturgy is expressed in the lives of those who perform.

Terrence is married with four children and seven grandchildren. He and his wife Linda reside in New Jersey, USA.

Rev. Terrence G Clark
The Glory Cloud publications
PO Box 193 Sicklerville NJ 08081
www.theglorycloudpublications.com
(Facebook) Voice of One Online
Vof1@aol.com
www.voicecnc.com (Magazine)

Richard Timbers II

FOR OTHER BOOKS BY THIS AUTHOR OR PUBLISHER VISIT THEGLORYCLOUDPUBLICATIONS.COM AMAZON, BARNES & NOBLE, VOICECNC.COM

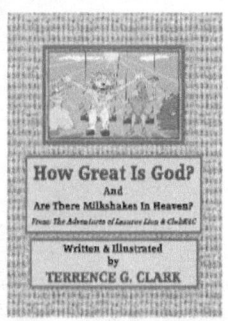

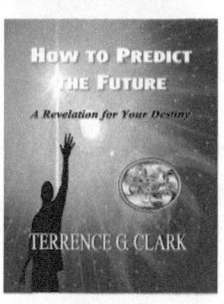

This book was published by:

The Glory Cloud publications LLC

P.O. Box 193

Sicklerville, NJ 08081

www.theglorycloudpublications.com

vof1@aol.com

For additional information about us and how to obtain other literature, or how to publish your life story, testimony, miracle report, biography, fiction, or children's story book, please write or email us at the above addresses.

Psalms 68:11
*Habakkuk 2:3, 4 *2 Corinthians 1-7*
**Jude 22*

With our Voice and His Glory, by Faith
Making a Difference in the World

The Story

Corinda, Candace, Ginger, Dori, and Diamond along with liturgical dance ministries from all over gather together on the East Coast (New Jersey) not only to dance in the annual competition, but to tell their stories. The stories of these girls, women, and men come together on stage as they perform before a collective, anticipative audience. Their lives proving that ministers of all gifting aren't perfect except when performing before the right audience.

Dancers read and take your ministry to the next level. As you will perhaps identify your own story in theirs. *Praise Dancer's Story* is must reading for anyone who is involved in liturgical dance—

Or, for anyone who has questions about its validity or place in worship. Or, for anyone who ministers in (or who is ministered to by) this *seemingly* new form of worship—liturgy.